Meg wante[d] ... body and take its heat like nourishment.

She wanted to run her hand down his back and learn the shape of his muscles and sinews and bones. She wanted to talk to him like a lover, tell him everything would be all right, Amy would be all right because she, Meg, was here with him and they'd each give the other the strength needed to get through anything that lay ahead, no matter how hard.

But that's impossible, she thought. We're not lovers, and we never will be. We're Amy's aunt and Amy's father, and the only thing we truly have in common is that we care about her.

And caring for a child could make a man ruthless....

Dear Reader,

♪♫ "Happy Birthday to us...." ♪♫ Exactly twenty years ago this May, Silhouette Romance was born. Since then, we've grown as a company, and as a series that continues to offer the very best in contemporary category romance fiction. The icing on the cake is this month's amazing lineup:

International bestselling author Diana Palmer reprises her SOLDIERS OF FORTUNE miniseries with *Mercenary's Woman*. Sorely missed, Rita Rainville returns to Romance with the delightful story of a *Too Hard To Handle* rancher who turns out to be anything but.... Elizabeth August delivers the dramatic finale to ROYALLY WED. In *A Royal Mission*, rescuing kidnapped missing princess Victoria Rockford was easy for Lance Grayson. But falling in love wasn't part of the plan.

Marie Ferrarella charms us with a *Tall, Strong & Cool Under Fire* hero whose world turns topsy-turvy when an adorable moppet and her enticing mom venture into his fire station.... Julianna Morris's BRIDAL FEVER! rages on when *Hannah Gets a Husband*—her childhood friend who is a new dad. And in *Her Sister's Child*, a woman allies with her enemy. Don't miss this pulse-pounding romance by Lilian Darcy!

In June, we're featuring Dixie Browning and Phyllis Halldorson, and in coming months look for new miniseries from many of your favorite authors. It's an exciting year for Silhouette Books, and we invite you to join the celebration!

Happy reading!

Mary-Theresa Hussey

Mary-Theresa Hussey
Senior Editor

Please address questions and book requests to:
Silhouette Reader Service
U.S.: 3010 Walden Ave., P.O. Box 1325, Buffalo, NY 14269
Canadian: P.O. Box 609, Fort Erie, Ont. L2A 5X3

HER SISTER'S CHILD

Lilian Darcy

ROMANCE™
Published by Silhouette Books
America's Publisher of Contemporary Romance

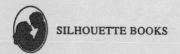

SILHOUETTE BOOKS

ISBN 0-373-19449-8

HER SISTER'S CHILD

Copyright © 2000 by Lilian Darcy

This edition published by arrangement with Harlequin Books S.A.

® and TM are trademarks of Harlequin Books S.A., used under license. Trademarks indicated with ® are registered in the United States Patent and Trademark Office, the Canadian Trade Marks Office and in other countries.

Visit Silhouette at www.eHarlequin.com

Printed in U.S.A.

Books by Lilian Darcy

Silhouette Romance

The Baby Bond #1390
Her Sister's Child #1449

LILIAN DARCY

Since her marriage to an irresistible New Yorker over ten years ago, Lilian Darcy has divided her time between various parts of the United States and her native Australia. Her children hold dual citizenship, and in her writing she tries to embody the shared strength of the two cultures—heroism, warmth and down-to-earth values. Although new to Silhouette, she has written over thirty books for the Harlequin Mills & Boon Medical Romance line and is now looking forward to creating strong, passionate stories for a whole new set of readers.

IT'S OUR 20ᵗʰ ANNIVERSARY!
We'll be celebrating all year,
Continuing with these fabulous titles,
On sale in May 2000.

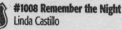

Chapter One

"**I**'m not going to lose my daughter!"

Adam Callahan muttered the words aloud and scowled up at the second-floor windows of the building he was headed for. The late April daylight was still strong, and behind the immaculate black-and-gold lettering on the pristine glass, he was certain he saw the vertical blinds move slightly.

Was he being watched? he wondered.

It wouldn't surprise him. He distrusted lawyers. Had he always distrusted them? Or was it only since last week, when he'd gotten the letter from Ms. Meg Jonas, Attorney at Law, Suite 201, 5608 West Broadbank Avenue, Philadelphia? It didn't matter. He distrusted *this* lawyer, and the people she represented. There was something cagey about her letter, something she was holding back, although the intentions of her clients were all too clear.

Easing his powerful black motorcycle backward so that the rear wheel nudged the curb, he muttered the words again, through clenched teeth this time. "I am *not* going to lose Amy!"

Now the statement had the force of a threat and the strength of a vow. There was desperation in it, too, when he thought of the other even darker fear that had been stalking him for the past few weeks, before he'd ever heard of Meg Jonas.

There was more than one way to lose a child, he reminded himself, while his heart seemed to lurch sideways in his chest. With Amy's life itself on the line, he *had* to play this whole thing right. He *needed* these people, far more than he would ever have wanted to need the people who were disputing his right to the custody of his own child.

If he hadn't needed them, he might have been able to dismiss them as he was convinced they deserved. He could have gotten a lawyer of his own to tell them just what they could do with their cruel and groundless custody claim. But as the situation stood now, and no matter how nasty things got later on, they'd all need to work together for the next few weeks with the common goal of Amy's well-being.

The only person who was out of the loop on the issue, as far as he was concerned, was this lawyer. He didn't care if he was over-reacting. She was a shark, breaking people's lives apart in return for her fat fee.

He was already ten minutes late for his meeting with the woman. It wasn't his choice. He'd been delayed at work and he'd tried hard to make up the time. He'd woven his way smoothly through the side streets and back alleys of Philadelphia on the bike. He'd calculated the likely peak hour traffic snarls in advance and avoided them as much as possible.

But now he rebelled. Let the lawyer woman wait a little longer! She and her clients were not about to get the idea that they had him on the run. They had no grounds for claiming custody of his daughter. None!

Unhurriedly, he pulled black leather gloves from his hands then began to unstrap his metallic black helmet. If Meg Jonas *was* watching him from her window, he'd give her a performance she wouldn't forget...

From her window, with a finger hooked around one slat of the blind to shift it two inches out of the way, Meg saw the leather-clad stranger shaking out his thick, dark hair. Although it was tidily cropped at the sides, it was long enough on top to need those lean fingers threading through it, putting the spring back into the waves.

Meg had heard the dying throb of the bike's engine a couple of minutes ago. Unnerved by the fact that he was late...unnerved by this whole situation, if she was honest...she'd gone over to the window with the deliberate aim of regaining control by getting an impression of Adam Callahan, assessing him before he had the chance to do the same to her.

He certainly wasn't in any hurry. Wasn't this meeting *important* to him, for heck's sake? It was to her, and to her parents. Painfully important...

He folded the gloves together and wadded them into the helmet, then started to unzip his leather jacket. He left the jacket on, but let it gape loosely to reveal a plain blue shirt that fitted smoothly over his broad chest. When he started on the black leather pants, twisting to reach the side zip and making the

leather stretch across his tightly muscled rear end before revealing dark gray trousers beneath, Meg felt an
involuntary shiver course the length of her spine.

Her sister Cherie had wanted this man, she remembered. Had apparently loved him enough to have a
child with him. It seemed totally out of character for
Cherie, but if Meg had put the dates together right,
the two of them must have been involved for over a
year before the inevitable split. That would have to
be a record. Cherie had never been able to stick to
anything for very long. Not a man, not a plan, not an
address.

Which was why Meg and her father had lost touch
with Cherie all during those crucial months of her
pregnancy. It was why they hadn't even *known* about
Cherie's child until Adam Callahan's letter to Dad in
California had arrived out of the blue two weeks ago.
But Cherie herself was dead...

Meg swallowed around the sudden lump in her
throat. Through no fault of her own, she had never
really known her sister. They had gone for months or
even years at a time with no contact. And for the past
six months it had been too late to change that. Cherie
was gone. But now, incredibly, they'd found that
Cherie had a baby daughter, living with a ratbag low-
life of a father, and this gave all of them a second
chance.

"A chance for Dad and me to do something for
Cherie's daughter that we could never do for Cherie
herself..." Meg murmured aloud, and it was almost
a prayer. A prayer for it all to work out.

How would Adam Callahan take the idea? Would
it come as a relief to him to give his baby over to a
pair of loving grandparents? Or did Meg and her fa-

ther and her new stepmom, Patty, have a battle brewing? Patty, in particular, had set her heart on this so much.

For a moment, with his leathers now bundled and locked in a black box attached near the back of the motorcycle, Adam Callahan didn't look quite so dark and menacing. His helmet was tucked innocently under his arm. His blue shirt and dark pants were conservative and well-fitting. But then he looked up at her window, almost as if he could see into her eyes, and there was such steel-hard anger and determination in his cleanly chiselled face that, for the second time, Meg shivered.

She'd suspected all along that this man must be dangerous. He'd been a danger to Cherie. He'd apparently involved her in a near-fatal motorcycle accident with his reckless driving, and that wasn't all.

What kind of a threat is he going to be to *me?* she wondered with an intuitive sense of dread.

"Get a grip, Meg!" she scolded herself aloud. "This is a business meeting, not a confrontation. Not yet, anyway. I'm a lawyer, acting for clients. Just because one of those clients happens to be my father... Oh, but maybe I should have listened to my very first instinct and not let Dad talk me into taking it on. I'm too close, too personally involved."

Searching for an emotional anchor, she looked around the office she was so proud of. She'd been in practice for just about seven months, since passing the Pennsylvania bar exam back in early September, but her client load was building steadily and already she'd tackled a couple of cases that were really satisfying. Nothing high-profile, no fat corporate fees or sensational court appearances, just wills and real estate closings and one fairly painless divorce.

But it was the work she had wanted to do, helping ordinary people with ordinary legal issues. She knew her clients were satisfied and several of them had said so. Word was getting around.

"But can I satisfy Dad and Patty? Can I satisfy myself? I wasn't ever planning to handle custody disputes. A case like this is completely different from what I know, and with my personal involvement..."

She heard footsteps on the stairs and knew it was Adam Callahan. Her receptionist in the outer office, Linda, had gone home half an hour ago. Maybe she shouldn't have suggested a meeting so late in the day, but she'd wanted to give it time, and she was committed to the confrontation now.

I'm not going to mess this up with what I feel, Meg vowed silently.

Smoothing the skirt of her teal-blue suit, she went to open the door.

Not what I expected.

That was Adam's first thought as he and the lawyer woman, Meg Jonas, shook hands and introduced themselves. Her fingers were warm and dry and fine, and her grip was like al dente spaghetti—firm without being brittle, just as a handshake should be. She offered him coffee, and her voice held a tiny thread of huskiness. Accepting automatically, although he didn't have the slightest desire for coffee—straight scotch might have suited his mood better—Adam found himself wondering if that husky note was always there or if it was just there today, now. He felt like his own voice might come out husky, too.

Because she was *definitely* not what he'd expected! He quickly tallied all the points of difference. Mid-twenties, when he'd assumed forties. Soft pink mouth and soft gray eyes, when he'd imagined a hard, bored face, glazed over with a well-fitting veneer of professional competence and good manners.

And pretty. He absolutely hadn't expected her to be so pretty. Lawyers just didn't come in packages like this, with heart-shaped faces and long dark lashes and dark hair, the color of some richly glinting rain-forest timber, waving softly around their shoulders. They weren't neat and petite in pretty blue suits and clinging white blouses, either. And they definitely didn't have full, bow-shaped lips perfectly painted in a subtle cinnamon-pink gloss.

Actually, her lips reminded him of someone. Someone important.

They were set firmly now, after her initial murmured greeting, but not as if the firmness came naturally. She was having to make an effort to stay calm, and he wondered why. He heard her clear her throat, saw those fine fingers tuck a strand of hair behind her ear. A moment later, the coffee was splashing untidily into the two cups she'd set out on the credenza, as if her hand wasn't quite steady.

And for the first time in weeks he didn't feel quite so hunted, or so despairing. There was something about this woman, something that soothed his suspicions and his bristling pain, something he instinctively wanted to respond to and trust. It was insane. It made no sense at all. But for the moment, feeling that he might actually have the upper hand, he went with that powerful gut instinct and let himself relax.

She had reached for the carton of cream now, her fine-boned hands still fluttering and distracted.

"No cream, thanks," he told her, but she'd already splashed some into her own cup and automatically moved the carton to hover over his.

He could almost hear her thoughts churning. From inside her own head, they must be deafening because she obviously hadn't heard what he'd said about the cream. He repeated it, and closed his hand lightly over hers just in time to stop the liquid from spilling over the tilted lip of the carton.

The moment of contact was strangely intimate. Her head whirled around to look up at him and he felt her start like a frightened animal. The feeling ran across into his own body like an electric current, and he took his hand away quickly, before something burst into flames. What was happening here?

"No cream?" she echoed, as if she'd never heard that coffee could be enjoyed that way.

"Or sugar," he told her patiently, hiding what he'd felt as their hands touched.

"Or sugar. Right. Neither do I."

"I guess I'm starting to understand why you became a lawyer," he drawled. Keep it light, Adam. Keep that upper hand.

She looked at him, even more startled this time. She'd moved away from him after their electric moment of physical contact and picked up a spoon. Now she plunged it into the hot black liquid and began to stir. She stammered, "Why? I mean..."

"Because you couldn't cut it as a waitress." He gave a half grin, waited for a fraction of a second and got his reward.

She laughed, a delighted, delightful sound. "You

got it," she said. "It's my secret tragedy. I can't serve coffee."

"And I can tell it's blighted your whole life. Here, give it to me before the cup goes into orbit."

"I beg your pardon?"

"Most people don't consider that black, sugarless coffee needs to be stirred quite that fast, or for quite that long."

"Oh. Right. I'm sorry. Should I start over?"

"Stirring doesn't actually *ruin* it, however."

"No..." She smiled, then sighed, and he saw the hunted look come back into her gray eyes again.

No, hunted wasn't the word. That was how *he* had felt lately. Hunted, and maybe already caught. Her eyes were more *haunted*. Sad. Grieving. Was she grappling with some difficult loss in her private life?

Adam, this is *not* your concern! he lectured himself. There's *nothing* about this woman's personal life you need to know or care about, and if she's nervous on top of whatever else is bothering her, so much the better. Use it!

Suddenly, all his wariness and latent hostility returned in full force, swamping that weird, intuitive chemistry between them and drowning it out completely.

"Where are the Fontaines?" he growled. He ignored the green leather chair she had ushered him toward, in her private office. "Shouldn't they be here, too? And what about Cherie? Where *is* she? What is this? I need some answers Ms. Jonas, and I intend to get them."

Mistake.

Why had he lost his cool like that, within a few minutes of their greeting? Well, he knew, of course.

His throat tightened as if an iron hand had gripped it. His baby. Amy was only fourteen months old, and already this was the fourth—count it, *the fourth!*— time he'd had to face the prospect of losing her. He had every reason in the world to blow his control, but unfortunately he couldn't plan to win this fight on a sympathy vote. He *had* to keep a clear head.

The lawyer woman slid into the neat little sage-toned office chair behind her walnut desk and he placed his coffee carefully on a coaster, then leaned his splayed hands on the smooth wood of the desk for a moment, still standing.

He looked down at her. He wasn't sorry that he appeared to tower over her from this position. He added quietly before she could reply to his initial tirade, "Your letter was very brief. And pretty short on facts. All I know is that you're acting for Cherie's parents, and they're claiming custody of my daughter. I'd like to know more."

He stepped back and sat down, forcing himself to take it slowly, and to think rather than simply act and feel. Feelings could be deceptive. Witness that uncanny electricity a few moments ago when their hands had touched.

Ms. Jonas had evidently decided to take things slowly, too, although he could tell that this was still far harder and more emotional for her than it should be.

"First," she said, then stopped, buying time with a sip of coffee. Her sensitive, sensual top lip looked fuller as it closed over the white china. "Do you have any legal representation of your own in this matter?"

Short answer. No. But should he bluff and say he did?

Adam decided on the simple truth. "Not yet. I'm hoping we can resolve this amicably, since I'm confident of my own claim to Amy and I have other priorities than this custody issue, when it comes to her well-being. I would have preferred if the Fontaines had written to me personally rather than bringing a lawyer in to mess with the situation before each of us even knows where the other is coming from."

Meg Jonas allowed herself a little smile, and he saw a glint of pearly white between those pretty pink lips. Lips that he was finding it hard to look away from. "You don't like lawyers?" she said.

"I didn't say that," he growled, bristling like a big cat.

"You didn't have to," she pointed out dryly, then took a deep, steadying breath. "Look, as you've said, I should clarify a few things first. For a start, my clients are not named Fontaine. It was a natural assumption on your part, since they're her parents, but Fontaine was Cherie's professional name, which she began using in child beauty pageants at the age of five. You need to know that I'm acting on behalf of Burt Jonas and his wife Patricia." She waited silently for a moment, correctly anticipating his reaction.

"Jonas?" he echoed. "But that's your—!"

"Yes," she nodded. "Burt Jonas is my father, Patty is my stepmother and Cherie is... Oh, damn...*was*...my younger sister."

"What do you mean 'was'?" Adam demanded hoarsely, his heart beginning to thud with sickening heaviness in his chest. Were those *tears* she was blinking back?

This was coming from way out in left field. Another tragedy, and, impossibly, yet another threat to

Amy. Aside from any other issues of grief and loss, if something had happened to Amy's closest blood relative, what did that do to her own chance of living?

"I'm sorry," Meg Jonas said, and it was clearly an effort for her. The words were jerking from her mouth. "We could tell from the wording of your letter to Dad, asking him to put you in touch with her, that you didn't know. Cherie was killed about six months ago, while on a modeling assignment in the Caribbean. A light plane crash. Another model, the photographer and the pilot all lost their lives. It was very difficult for Dad. It still is. For over a year, he hadn't known where she was, what she was doing, how to reach her..."

"That sounds like Cherie," Adam agreed shakily. "I had the same problem with her more than once."

"She was... erratic," Meg agreed. "We all know that. But then, within weeks of her getting in touch again and letting us know, at last, that she was doing fine and getting her modeling career back on track, came her death."

Adam swore softly. "It must have been—I mean, dammit, even for me it's—"

Meg Jonas nodded silently, and they both sat for what must have been several minutes, wrapped in difficult thoughts. She was the one to speak first. "Mr. Callahan, I—"

"Doctor," he corrected automatically, staring into the distance.

"*Dr.* Callahan? You're a doctor? A practising medical doctor?"

"Yes." He looked up. "A third-year resident in pediatrics. Why? Is that a surprise?" he demanded.

She was leaning forward, examining him with unnerving intensity.

"Yes," she admitted bluntly. "I— A couple of things Cherie said about you…"

"Cherie told you about me?" Now *he* was surprised. Their involvement had only lasted about two months. Just a fleeting blip on Cherie's emotional radar screen.

"Not much," Meg Jonas said.

"But nothing about Amy?"

"No. Until Dad got your letter two weeks ago, we had no idea she had had a baby. Absolutely no idea. She never said a word. Another shock." The faint, tired smile didn't reach those pretty eyes.

"Too many of them," Adam agreed. His thoughts swirled in his brain like bats in a cave, and he knew that for Cherie's sister, perhaps the biggest shock was still to come…when he judged the time was right to deliver it.

"Far too many," Meg said. "I never felt I knew Cherie very well." She was speaking slowly, staring down at her desk so that he couldn't see her gray eyes, just her thick creamy lids edged by those dark lashes.

"Mom and Dad split up when I was eight and Cherie was three," she went on.

Adam listened, amazed. Lawyers didn't bare their souls like this, to someone on the opposite side of the legal fence from their own client. But it was obvious by now that this wasn't a situation this particular lawyer had been in before. And as for Adam himself…

"They agreed they'd each take one of us. I went with Dad," she said, "while Cherie stayed with Mom. I've always felt guilty about that."

"Guilty?"

"I got the better deal. I don't know if she told you much about her childhood..."

"Bits," Adam replied. "Like jigsaw puzzle pieces. Snatches of color and tone that I couldn't ever put together as well as I wanted, because she never gave me the whole picture."

Again, Meg gave that faint, weary smile. "That's Cherie. Mom was the same. Constantly in search of some new dream, but never slowing down long enough to explain to anyone quite what it was. It took her all over the country, with Cherie in tow, moving once, even twice a year. Dad got frantic at first. He never knew, when he called, if the phone would be disconnected. He never knew if his plans to see Cherie during school vacations would get cancelled at the last minute because they'd moved on again and hadn't given us the new address. At some point, I think, he gave up." She stopped.

"Gave up?" Adam prompted. He was learning an incredible amount about this complex, sensitive woman just from the way she was telling the story. He could feel his attitude and his emotions changing every minute. Right now, he was too caught up in Meg's words to think about what that really meant.

"Kind of encased his love for Cherie in a thick layer of cement so it couldn't do him damage. Like nuclear waste, or something." She spread her fine hands helplessly, as if asking him to indulge the clumsy comparison.

"I think I understand."

"It just hurt too much," she went on. "He's an organized, sensible man, while my Mom—she died several years ago—was..." She looked up again, and this time her smile was wider, though just as complicated. The wisdom in what she said belonged to someone much older. "Well, let's just say, don't let anyone tell you that opposites attract!"

"No?" Adam was thinking of Cherie. Cherie and himself and that first, chance meeting of theirs in a Philadelphia shopping mall. A disastrous quirk of fate in so many ways, yet how could he wish it had never happened? He *couldn't.*

"Well, okay, maybe they do attract," Meg conceded. "In the beginning. That was the case with Mom and Dad, at first, and they were as opposite as it comes. But opposites can't make it last, when it comes to a relationship."

"That, I agree with."

"So I grew up not knowing my sister, and hardly knowing my mom. It was…incredible to find out that Cherie had a child. How did you track Dad down? We were confused, at first, because you'd gotten the name wrong, and all."

My turn to bare my soul, Adam thought.

But some instinct told him not to, just yet, not fully. For a start, he definitely wasn't going to talk about Amy's illness yet, and what she needed. There was time for that, and it was too important to get it wrong. He distrusted this lawyer, he reminded himself firmly. Despite the endearing fact that she couldn't serve coffee and that she could speak to a stranger like him from the heart.

Scratch the surface, and she was probably cut from the same cloth as his former college roommate, Garry, who seduced my girlfriend behind my back and then laughed when I found out and told me to "join the real world," he remembered.

The guy was a celebrity defense lawyer now. "The guiltier my clients, the happier I'll be," he used to say. "They'll pay more that way."

For this woman, did it come down to money, too?

"I needed to get in touch with Cherie," he said, deliberately avoiding detail. "But I didn't know how. I tried her old modeling agency, but they hadn't kept any records and they didn't want to know. They weren't exactly a top-flight establishment. They only had a few staff members to handle all their clients and their wannabes. And I think they'd written Cherie off."

"Perhaps a few of us had," she came in quietly. "You, too?"

"I...didn't think to try a bigger, better agency, no," Adam admitted. "After Amy was born...or even before...Cherie seemed like she was headed on the opposite trajectory. Down, not up."

"I know," Meg nodded. "That was the one thing that made her death easier for Dad. That she'd turned her life around. That she died doing what she had wanted to do, and was on the edge of real success."

"So I was just about to put the whole thing in the hands of a private investigator. I even wondered if she might be living on the streets."

"I know," Meg nodded again. "We've had those fears, too, in the past."

"Then I was flipping through an old notepad by my phone and I caught sight of her handwriting, and there it was. Just a scribble. It had to be well over a year old, and I could hardly read it. 'Dad in 'Frisco after November 1st.' Something like that, followed by his address. She hadn't mentioned him often. I didn't know if she was still in touch with him. But it seemed like the best lead I had, so I tried it. I just addressed it to 'Mr. Fontaine.' I never knew Fontaine was only Cherie's professional name.''

"Her legal one, too, for most of her life. Mom had it changed officially when she was seven. It was meant to help Cherie's modeling career, as well.''

"Part of Amy's name, too. Amy Fontaine Callahan." He said the "Callahan" part with deliberate emphasis, claiming his child. Amy was a Callahan, and she would stay a Callahan. *His*.

Was the pretty lawyer, Cherie's sister, trying to soften him up? Of course she was! He distrusted her. He must not lose sight of that fact. He'd trusted Cherie at first, too, believing that she was as bright and sincere and in control of her life as she'd then seemed.

They didn't look alike, the two sisters. They had the same mouth, that was all. Cherie had been model-perfect, with a lifetime of training in how to be beautiful, thanks to the roll call of pageants her mother had pushed her through for years. By twenty, when he'd met her—although initially she'd lied and told him she was twenty-four—she had a model's tall, lean build, wide sultry eyes, carefully graceful movements and gorgeous, pouting mouth.

Yes, Meg definitely had the same mouth. The rest of her was different, though. She wasn't blond. She wasn't as tall, and she wasn't as lean. Her blue suit covered some very feminine curves. And you couldn't really say she was beautiful. These days, beauty wasn't an innocent quality, and in Meg Jonas's unstudied prettiness, there was an unmistakable innocence.

Hey…

Adam pulled himself up short. What was happening to him? Who was he kidding, here? This woman? Innocent? She was a lawyer! She practised a profession that could draw the cynics and hard-hearts and opportunists of this world like blood drew sharks. She was Cherie's sister, under her very different skin. And she was trying to win his daughter away from him.

So he'd better keep that fact firmly in the center of his mind. She was no innocent.

Okay, so maybe everything Meg had said so far was true. All that feeling spilled from her pretty lips and that suffering in her big gray eyes. But it was still a game, part of a strategy and a plan. Her dad wanted custody, and she was acting for him.

Adam understood a little more now about how Burt Jonas must feel. A chance to regain his lost daughter through her child. Yes, Adam understood the power of that hope. But had Meg Jonas deliberately tried to foster this empathy in him in order to strengthen the Jonases' claim?

I'm the one that endured those weeks in the hospital after Amy's premature birth, when her doctors thought that she might not make it, he reminded himself, while his hands tightened into fists.

I'm the one who endured it when Cherie took her for nearly three months and disappeared. *I'm* the one Cherie left her with when she disappeared again, leaving only that scribbled note in Amy's diaper bag. "Adam, you take her. I can't deal with her anymore."

I'm the one who's had her for the nine months since Cherie abandoned her: caring for her, loving her, watching her learn and grow.

And I'm the one who had to face those test results four-and-a-half weeks ago, telling me my baby girl is seriously ill...

Chapter Two

Meg hadn't missed the steel in Adam Callahan's voice when he said his daughter's full name, and she knew that Dad and Patty were kidding themselves if they thought this man would give his little girl up without a fight.

Hell, she'd been kidding herself in the exact same way a week and a half ago when she'd drafted the legal letter she'd sent to him, after what seemed like hours of phone calls between herself here in Philly and Dad and Patty in San Francisco, talking about what they wanted. They'd still been reeling from the revelation that Cherie had had a child.

She wasn't kidding herself anymore.

The trouble was, Adam Callahan was nothing at all like what she had imagined. Nothing at all like Cherie had described, one of only two times they'd spoken about him together, nearly two years ago. The phone call from her sister was carved into her memory. It had come out of the blue after the usual months of silence, made from some gas station phone booth in a midwestern town whose name Meg couldn't even remember. Maybe Cherie hadn't been that specific. Somewhere in Indiana?

She'd sounded wild that night. Giggly. Happy. In love. Out of control. Some guy on a motorcycle who sounded dangerous and bad. She'd called him by some in-your-face nickname. Slash?

"He's in trouble with the law, but I don't care. He takes me places, Meg, heights I didn't know existed. He makes me quiver. My modeling? That's meaningless. I just want to be with him, travelling, forever, on the back of his bike, feeling the air. I don't care about anything else. And neither does he..."

The second time Cherie had talked about him was over a year later, and this time she'd made more sense, seemed more grounded. The guy had turned out to be "bad news." He'd "nearly killed" her in a motorcycle smash, then walked away. A lot had happened...Baby Amy, for one thing, although typically Cherie hadn't mentioned that. Who could fathom her motives there? She'd just claimed vaguely that Meg didn't need the details... But finally, "I realized he wasn't going to change." She had signed with a new, much better agency and she was getting back into modeling. The guy was history.

None of that sounded like the man who sat in Meg's office right now. Oh, Adam Callahan looked like a man who could make a woman quiver, all right. No problem there. And he rode that big black motorcycle.

But the rest of it didn't gel. He was a doctor, and he wasn't just some guy who fathered a child with a woman then shrugged off the responsibility and moved on. It was already very apparent that he was passionate about keeping his little girl. Look at the suppressed tension in him now! The power of it mocked the carefully chosen decor of Meg's office.

She was proud of the restful, creative touches she'd given to her work environment. The shelf of knick-knacks, mainly hand-carved Inuit animals in wood and stone. The botanical prints with their earthy, natural colors. The soft, comfortable leather of the sage-green chairs.

But the strength of what Adam Callahan felt and the strength of who he was as a man made this office suddenly feel like a prison, and Meg couldn't even pretend to herself that she was fully in control anymore. It had begun the moment she saw him, and continued during that disturbing instant when their hands had touched over the coffee. The sense of a connection that went beyond logic and reason.

Now her heart was racing. She had no clue as to how she would report this meeting to Dad and Patty, even though she knew they'd both be hovering by their phone in San Francisco tonight, waiting for her call. And she had a growing suspicion that there was something vital Adam was holding back, the most potent ingredient of all in this sizzling emotional mix.

They'd both been silent now for more than a minute. She sipped her rapidly cooling coffee, just for something to do with her mouth and hands, then saw that he was gulping his for the same reason. His eyes, almost as dark as the bitter black drink, were narrowed and he was thinking, calculating.

Thoughts that were painful, almost desperate, if his expression was any guide. There were lines scored from each corner of his mouth, and tight little balls of muscle at his jaw. Lines of strain around his eyes, too.

And she had the most impossible need, suddenly, to go over to him, kneel in front of him, take his head in her hands and smooth away all that tension with her fingers. Crazy! She was already far too involved emotionally, with her own side of this brewing custody dispute. To feel anything but the strictest professional distance and neutrality about Adam Callahan would be a nightmare!

She forced herself to ignore what she could read in his face. Instead, she took another shaky sip of her coffee, then watched as he brought his own cup to his lips once more. His hands were strong and lean and well-kept as a doctor's had to be. They were folded around the thick white cup as if he needed the heat, yet it wasn't cold in here. In fact, Meg herself felt steamy hot in her suit, and very conscious of the state of her body.

For her own protection, this silence had to be broken, and broken soon!

"How long had you been trying to track Cherie down, then?" she asked quickly, then added, "No wait! Can we go further back? How long since you lost contact with her in the first place? I'm not clear at all about the progression of your relationship."

He laughed harshly. "I don't think there was a progression. Or a relationship. We were only together, truly, for a couple of months."

"A couple of months?" Meg echoed, fighting to keep her voice neutral. This didn't remotely gel with what Cherie had said, but if she'd caught Adam Callahan out in a lie she didn't want him to realize the fact. "Okay..." she added blandly, inviting him to go on.

He did, wrapped up in remembering. She controlled a sigh of relief. He hadn't guessed that she'd spotted his inconsistency, which gave her time to think—frantically, without answers—about what the inconsistency meant.

"She disappeared within a month of us discovering she was pregnant," he said. "Wouldn't consider marriage."

"You *wanted* to? *You* did?" Again Meg tried to hide her disbelief.

Not very successfully this time. He looked up. "Yes. For a while. For Amy's sake. Until I saw how impossible it would be. Why? What did Cherie tell you?"

"Nothing." Nothing that meshed with Adam's story, anyway. And she had to remind herself, as she was reminding Adam, "I had no contact with her at that time, remember?" And Cherie was adept at changing her stories as time went by. Maybe it wasn't Adam Callahan who'd got it wrong...

No! Why am I feeling this need to find ways to trust him?

"Then what are you—" he began.

"I'm implying nothing." She fudged quickly. "I guess it doesn't fit the stereotype, that's all. Usually, it's the woman who wants marriage and security for her child, while the man ducks it with every strategy he can think of."

There was a tell-tale beat of silence. "You're a lawyer. I keep forgetting," Adam said with a snort. "Cynical is your middle name." He hadn't thought about Garry in recent years, but even in hindsight, the guy's attitude still stank.

"It's not cynicism." She bristled. "It's statistics. I don't like those statistics any more than you seem to. I'm—well, impressed that you have such a responsible, caring attitude, okay?"

"Okay," he conceded.

And maybe it *was* okay for him. Meg herself was horrified. She'd practically given him a medal of honor, let him know straight out how much he was rising in her estimation. In other words, she'd just kissed goodbye her last vestige of professionalism.

One of the key arguments in her dad's planned custody claim for his only granddaughter was always going to be that Amy's biological father was unfit to care for a child. Less than an hour ago, that had seemed quite a reasonable assumption, with the mental picture she and Dad and Patty had built of Adam Callahan, based on Cherie's extravagant, erratic words.

But the reality was turning out to be so different...

Just get off the subject before it eats this whole case alive. Move on. Knowledge is power, so get some *facts,* Meg coached herself inwardly. Mentally, she back-tracked, while wondering just why she was finding it so difficult to keep her focus in Adam Callahan's presence. Even now, filled with renewed determination and hostility, she kept noticing the way he tapped his foot rhythmically and silently on the floor, unconsciously drawing attention to the lean, strong length of his legs.

But that *wasn't* what she was supposed to be thinking about! "So your relationship didn't last long?" she asked, trying to get a handle on the timing, at least. This definitely wasn't what she'd understood from Cherie.

"No," he answered. "Or not as far as I was concerned. Cherie disappeared, then turned up again begging for another chance when she was nearly six months pregnant." Adam was simplifying it a little. Cherie had actually run out on him twice. "I gave it to her," he went on. "I tried. And while she needed me, while her pregnancy was slowing her down and keeping her out of action, it was okay. I was at Amy's birth, which was great...amazing...terrifying."

"Terrifying?"

He met her challenging look. "I guess you don't know that Amy was a couple of months premature. She was in hospital for weeks, and it was touch and go whether she'd be okay."

"No," Meg answered starkly. "You're right. I didn't know."

But she could see in the man's face even now what Amy's difficult start had cost him. How old was he, exactly? Only in his early thirties, surely, yet there were lines of strain etched around his eyes and mouth.

"I spent my whole life at the hospital," he went on. "Between doing my pediatric residency there and being with Amy. Cherie wasn't interested. Anyway, I didn't even know where she was. So I started making plans to raise Amy myself. But the day before she was ready for discharge from the hospital, Cherie just came and took her, and for two and a half months I had no idea what had happened to either of them. Until my brother's wedding day last July. My new sister-in-law found Amy just lying on the bed in my parents' spare room, with her diaper bag all packed. Baby formula. A couple of outfits. And a note from

Cherie saying she couldn't handle her anymore and Amy was mine. It was the last I ever heard from her, and Amy never saw her mom again.''

''But you waited nine months to try and find Cherie?'' Meg asked, deliberately applying the pressure. There *had* to be an inconsistency here, if not a downright lie, and she was determined to understand it.

''Yes,'' he nodded, then took a deep, controlled breath. ''You see—''

But she didn't let him finish, and attacked openly. ''What, because now *you* 'couldn't handle it' and were hoping it was Cherie's turn? Is this baby of yours like a tennis ball to you, or something? You think it's fine if she just gets batted back and forth?''

Okay, Meg, she coached herself again as she watched Adam and waited for the building explosion. This level of anger and hostility wasn't particularly professional, either, but it was the best she could do. Far better than feeling her heart go out to him as she understood more and more every minute about what he must have been through over the past year and a half, and more.

As she'd expected after her accusations, he was struggling for control. What she hadn't expected was that he would win the struggle. But he did.

''I didn't try to get in touch with Cherie for nine months,'' he answered her quietly, ''because, from experience, I didn't think any input from Cherie in Amy's life would be good for her.''

''No? Her own *mother?*''

''Yes, a mother who disappeared and came back again without warning, and whose plans went from green to red and back again in the space of twenty-four hours. Even if Cherie had gone on to have the success she deserved and was starting to find as a model, I doubt that aspect of her character would ever have changed,'' he argued forcefully. ''Kids need continuity. I believe that. Maybe you don't. *Obviously*, you don't, if you're prepared to—''

He broke off, and Meg didn't know why he'd suddenly thought better about completing his sentence. She could have completed it for him, and once again had to fight the idea that there was truth in it. *Was* she prepared to work toward taking a little girl from the only parent she had ever known?

But this is what he *wants*, the inner legal coach reminded her. Of course he wants to trick you into seeing it all from his point of view! You only have his word on *any* of this, that any of it happened the way he says it did. People will go to any lengths when it comes to custody, legal or illegal. Lying is par for the course. Some people kidnap their own children and take them out of the country. And where are his facts? How do I know he is who he says he is? Meg Jonas, do not concede one inch to this man yet!

''Anyway,'' Adam growled now. ''This is all irrelevant.'' He laughed, but it didn't seem like he truly thought that there was anything funny in the situation. It was an almost painful sound, his laughter, straining tightly through his throat.

''What's irrelevant?'' Meg questioned, needing to challenge him further.

''The whole issue of who gets custody of Amy.''

''*Irrelevant?*'' She was right! He did have some devious thing going. She'd sensed all along that he was holding something back.

Suddenly, she felt sick at how close she'd come to

trusting him, falling for his lines, even...yes, she could admit it now...thinking that she could be *attracted* to him. "Irrelevant?" she repeated on a furious squeak, rising from behind the deceptive protection of her desk to pace the office and claim it for herself again. He had dominated the space too much today.

"What on earth are we here for, what has this all been *about,* if custody of Amy is irrelevant? I can assure you, Dr. Callahan, in the strongest possible terms, that to my father and stepmother the issue of who has the right, the *legal* right, to raise and care for Amy Fontaine Callahan is the most relevant issue in their lives at this time, and will remain that way until the matter is settled to their satisfaction."

"You're wrong about that," he answered, his deep voice suddenly sounding inexpressibly weary. "But of course you can't understand it yet."

"Understand what?" she snapped.

"Look, there's something I haven't told you."

"Really? Then tell me now. If there are facts pertaining to this case that—"

"Yes. Of course. Spare me the legalese, okay?" Still that weariness which dominated and shadowed his voice. "It's after six, and I don't want to discuss this in your office. It isn't a professional matter."

"It isn't?" Her mind was whirling now. What game was he playing? He was on his feet now, close enough for her to feel his pull on her senses. He *couldn't* be hoping to seduce her into any sort of concession, could he?

"No," he answered, his dark gaze boring into her eyes. "It's about as personal as you can get. So can we get out of here? I want to take you to dinner."

* * *

Why am I here? Why on earth did I agree to this?

Adam could see her thinking it as they sat at an intimate corner table in the Italian restaurant she'd nominated, waiting for their drinks to arrive.

She had argued at first, bristling and indignant and trying very hard to stay professional. Dinner? With him? Absolutely not! Without wanting to, he found himself smiling at the memory, and had to cover his mouth with his hand to hide it, pretending to scratch his nose.

She was incredibly...*interesting*...when she was angry, he decided, deliberately picking the safest word he could think of. She unconsciously stretched straighter to try and make more of her modest height, so that her neat, rounded breasts thrust forward, vying for prominence with her determined chin. Her eyes shot hot sparks, although cool gray eyes like hers ought not to have any fire in them at all. Her voice rose, and her vocabulary leaned heavily on her years at law school. Outside of the hospital, he hadn't heard so many multisyllabic words in one sentence in a long time.

And he didn't quite know how he'd finally talked her round. Didn't remember what he'd said. He only knew that he'd fought for it with all the tenacity he had because it was crucial...literally a matter of life and death...that he and Meg Jonas get past their mutual hostility over the custody issue so he could tell her about Amy and ask her to look at making a bigger sacrifice for his little girl than she'd probably ever needed to make for anyone before in her life.

Well, he'd carried his point somehow. She'd finally stopped her indignant arguing, searched his face with

shimmering, troubled eyes then murmured something
about Lorenzo's Trattoria and him following her car
on his motorcycle. They'd both been so distracted that
she hadn't waited for him to put on his leather gear,
and he hadn't even thought of it, and now they were
here and his body was still warming up after the chilly
five minute ride in the rapidly cooling April evening.

"What is this *about*, Dr. Callahan?" she burst out
as soon as her drink arrived.

He hadn't taken in what she'd ordered, but it was
long and cold and the glass was already beading with
moisture. The way she held it, her fingers left five
neat oval prints on the wetness when she took a sip
and put the glass down again.

He took a slug of his beer before he answered her,
still playing for time. Gut instinct told him that he
had to establish at least a semblance of rapport with
her before he answered her question properly.

"Let's eat first," he said.

But she wasn't having that. "No! I've already
given you more than enough latitude in this. You
claim you've got something to say. Something that
changes the whole situation. Well, I want to hear it!
Now! And if I don't, then I'm going to walk right out
of here." Her index finger stabbed in the direction of
the door. "And the next step *you'll* need to take will
be to find yourself a good attorney to handle your
side of the case."

"Okay, okay." Unfortunately, he could see that
she wasn't bluffing. Why should she? She had nothing to lose by maintaining their antagonism.

Or rather, he amended to himself, she *thought* she
had nothing to lose.

But she was wrong. She had Amy to lose. And that

was his greatest asset, he realized, because it meant that even if he did have to tell her the cruel facts now, bluntly, with no lead in, she just might understand.

Their waiter appeared, and Adam waved him away. "Not yet," he said. "Give us a few minutes, okay?"

"No problem."

Adam waited until the man was out of earshot, then just bit the bullet and came out with it as simply as he could. The words, as usual, tasted bitter and painful and impossible in his mouth.

"Amy is ill, Ms. Jonas. She has leukemia."

"Leukemia!"

He saw the shocked widening of her eyes, and went on urgently, "She needs a bone marrow donor, and if we can find someone compatible, then she should…she *will*…recover completely. But if there's no one… That's why I needed to contact Cherie so urgently. I'm not a good match, and neither is anyone in my family. We all got tested when we heard of her illness, but it just didn't work out. Cherie was our only hope, and even though she wasn't the best mother in the world—hell, we both know that!—I know she would have done it.

"When you told me just now that she'd been killed… You know we weren't involved long enough or deeply enough for me to carry a life-long grief over that, but my little girl…if I lost her…"

"Yes…"

"I thought she'd lost her best chance when you gave me the news, until I thought about the fact that you and Cherie were sisters. Would you be willing to do it? To get tested? And, if you're compatible, donate your bone marrow to my baby?"

Chapter Three

"Dad, sorry it's so late. I know you've been waiting for me to call," Meg said into the phone, just moments after she arrived home that night.

Her father had picked up on the first ring. Now he didn't waste words. "Okay, shoot, Meggie. Did it go well? Was he what we were expecting?"

The two impossible questions she had known he would ask. She had the answers prepared, but her throat suddenly felt dry all the same. Unbearably so. She went into the galley-style kitchen of her one bedroom apartment with the cordless phone pressed between her shoulder and her ear and got some sparkling mineral water from the fridge. She spoke as she went. Carefully.

"No, he wasn't what we were expecting. I can't go into any details yet." She took a big gulp of the mineral water and her parched mouth felt better.

"You're calling from your office? He can't still be with you..."

"No, I'm calling from home. I'm alone."

"Then why can't you talk?"

"Because I want to be cautious about this, Dad. There's…more going on than we realized." A lot more. "It'll be a few days before I can really be clear about what's happening."

There was a clatter in her ear and the sound of Patty's warm voice. "Meg, I have to know. Your dad's asking all the wrong questions. Is this Callahan man a total low-life, or not? Did you see Amy?"

Answer the easy one first. "No, I didn't see her. She was staying with his mother overnight."

"His *mother?* Men like that don't have mothers! Not ones you can safely leave a baby with, anyway."

"He's not a 'man like that,' Patty," she had to say. "Or if he is, he's a darn good liar."

"Of course he's a good liar! Men like that *are!*"

"And he's not going to give Amy up easily. I don't even know if—"

"But we can win it, right? Her own grandparents? Financially secure, with me giving up work as soon as she's with us, so I can care for her full-time? And after everything Cherie said about him? Oh, I'm just aching for that poor little girl, and what she must have to endure!"

"I know." Meg was aching, too. For different reasons.

She managed to deflect another five minutes of questions and finally put down the phone, exhausted by the effort of holding back what she knew. She wasn't going to frighten Dad or Patty with the specter of Amy's leukemia.

Not yet. Not until she'd satisfied herself that this

whole thing wasn't just some sick scam, and that
Adam Callahan was really the man he said he was.

She didn't know why the issue of trusting him was
building such conflict inside her. Was it a lawyer's
instinct? A lawyer's caution? Those things had been
drummed into her constantly through three years of
law school and she put them into practice daily in her
legal work now.

Even a simple real estate closing could turn into a
minefield of problems. People lied. Just last month,
she'd saved some clients from handing over every
penny they'd put away to a man who was trying to
sell them a house he didn't even own. He was a plau-
sible character, too. Attractive and sophisticated.

Yes, there were people out there who deliberately,
brazenly, *believably* lied, and for a dozen different
reasons. Financial gain, self-preservation, easy sex...
Was it *just* her lawyer's instinct to fear that Adam
Callahan might be one of them?

Restless, she downed the last inch of her mineral
water and wandered into the bathroom to wash hands
that felt clammy with tension, then caught sight of
her flushed face in the mirror.

She'd resorted to a glass of wine over dinner in an
attempt to stay cool and focused as they discussed
Amy's illness. It hadn't worked. But she knew it
wasn't the wine bringing this color to her face. It was
Adam Callahan.

She couldn't remember when any man had had
such a powerful, immediate effect on her senses, or
on her emotions. It wasn't just his dark, lively good
looks. She'd never been instantly susceptible to good-
looking men, so it *couldn't* be that. What was it, then?
The apparent strength of his feelings? His determi-

nation? His way of listening, with those black-coffee eyes of his fixed on her, liquid and intent, and his well-drawn mouth serious and sensitive?

"Oh, boy, he really did a number on me tonight, didn't he?" she muttered to her reflection. "He probably got *exactly* what he wanted. I swallowed every word he told me and started treating him like a hero."

She saw that flushed cheeks weren't the only difference in her appearance tonight. Her eyes shone, her breathing was shallower than usual, and even her lips looked fuller. Swollen. As if they'd been kissed. Which they hadn't.

But she'd *wanted* him to.

Oh, lord, might as well be completely honest about it! By the end of the evening she'd hardly been able to drag her gaze from his mouth as he talked. Then, when they'd said goodnight outside the restaurant, after arranging to meet at the hospital tomorrow for her blood test, she'd actually swayed toward him for one tell-tale second before getting a grip on her physical response to him.

But maybe he hadn't noticed, she prayed now. Maybe he'vd been distracted, because I'd finally gotten him to agree to my meeting Amy tomorrow, after the blood test.

He hadn't wanted the meeting, she recalled. Why? That was strange, wasn't it? Suspicious?

"No, I *don't* trust him!" she told the mirror forcefully aloud. "I really don't!"

Saying it so decisively like that felt like taking control at last, and she sensed her body beginning to unwind from its state of coiled tension. To her surprise, after a mug of hot chocolate and the late TV news, she actually slept soundly.

* * *

He was afraid I wouldn't show.

Meg could see this at once. He was waiting for her outside the Pathology department of the hospital where he worked, prowling restlessly. She had seen him just seconds before he looked along the corridor to see her. The relief in him when he did was totally apparent and sincere. His big, hunched shoulders relaxed, his dark eyes opened wider, his mouth softened like summer fruit ripening and he actually smiled.

Cautiously.

"I should have told you where to park," he said, not wasting energy on a hello.

"I'm a big girl," she answered. "I managed."

"And how do you feel about needles?"

"I feel fine about them," she claimed, waving a confident hand, then admitted, "So long as they're going up and down through a piece of fabric."

"So maybe you're not such a big girl, after all?"

They both laughed, though it wasn't a particularly joyous sound. He touched her briefly on the shoulder. She felt the lingering warmth of his hand through the fine knit of her sweater. Their awareness of each other was almost painful. She'd never imagined the possibility of such a complex mix of emotions about one man. Empathy. Distrust. Attraction...

"Through here," he said. "It's just a simple blood test, in your arm. They know what they're doing. It'll bite a little when the needle goes in, but if you look away..."

"I think I can handle it, Dr. Callahan."

"Can we please use first names, at least!"

"Is that wise? Shouldn't we keep—"

He turned to her and gripped her upper arm, chafing it in a rough caress that he wasn't even aware of. *She* was, though. Why did it feel so good just to be close to him? Was it just that he seemed so solid and strong?

"Look," he said, "If you're referring to the custody issue and the fact that we're on opposite sides of the fence...then don't! I can't deal with that right now! I want my little girl to live. That's the only thing that matters to me, and surely it matters to you, too! She's your niece. Do you ever think of that?" The accusation mounted in his tone.

"Of course it matters! Of course I think of it."

"Then do me a favor. Pretend we're friends. Think about the fact that we're on the same side right now, no matter what happens later on. I *need* you, Meg. Amy needs you."

"I—I know."

"And if you're a compatible donor then you're going to need me. Or need *someone* for support, anyway. It's not an easy process to go through."

"I know nothing about it," she admitted. "Last night we only talked about the blood test."

And I wasn't sure, then, that any of this was real, she added inwardly. I'm sure now...

"Maybe that's as far as we should take it for now," he suggested.

"You're scaring me. What exactly is involved?"

"No, sorry." He released her arm at last, but the appeal remained in his face. "That's not what I meant to do. I'm talking to myself, I guess. Telling myself to take it one step at a time. If you're not compatible with Amy..." His voice was husky.

"One step at a time." She nodded slowly. "You're

right. We can't think too far ahead. Let's just get this part done."

Drawing the blood took only a minute or two. Taking his advice, she didn't watch, just distracted herself by reading the humorous cartoons and sayings thumbtacked on the walls.

"I used to take life one day at a time," read one of them, "but lately a whole flock of days have attacked me at once."

Strangely appropriate, somehow. If Adam had been in the room, she would have pointed it out to him, but when he'd asked if she wanted him there for support, it seemed too weak to say yes...or maybe she just hadn't wanted him to hear if she yelled in pain!...so he was waiting outside.

"There, all done now," said the medical technician cheerfully as she gently withdrew the needle. "Results in a week to ten days."

"Okay. Thanks."

A minute later, Meg had a circle of flesh-colored Band-Aid stuck in the crook of her left arm and was out in the waiting area where Adam sat. He had a magazine open in front of him. A fishing magazine. It wasn't hard to tell that he hadn't read a word of it. He flung it back on the pile and said lightly, "I didn't hear any screams."

"I screamed silently. Figured people would be grateful if I spared their hearing."

"Considerate."

"Very," she agreed. "Seriously, though, it was fine. I haven't had a needle in years, and I was expecting it to be a lot worse. She said the results would—"

"I know," he nodded quickly.

"Of course. You're a doctor. I keep forgetting."

"Good. Let's forget *all* of this, okay?" He was pep-talking himself as much as appealing to her. "Nothing more can happen until we find out the results. So for now I'm taking you to meet Amy."

They both knew it was important, but somehow, by unworded agreement, they tried hard to pretend it wasn't. That it was just an ordinary visit, one they both wanted, rather than one he'd tried hard to postpone. Meg still wondered about his reasons for that.

The glorious spring day helped in the illusion that they were in agreement, that this was a casual event.

"Can we take your car? Then, if you could, drop me back at the hospital later on?" he asked her casually as they left the main building and felt the brilliant strike of the spring sunshine. "My car's here, and I have to work tonight."

"Your car? What about the motorcycle?" It came out almost like an accusation, and she realized that she was still clinging to that bad boy image of him, conjured by Cherie's words months ago. It hadn't occurred to her that he might drive something so tame and civilized as a car, as well.

He looked at her sharply. "You didn't notice I didn't have my helmet with me?"

"Unobservant, I guess." She shrugged, trying to make light of it.

"I used the motorcycle yesterday because I wanted the quickest way of getting between the hospital and your office in the traffic, since timing was tight, but mostly I don't use it now." He added deliberately, "It's merely a relic of my wild youth."

And she walked right into the trap. "You had a wild youth?"

He pounced. "You hope so, don't you? That's what you're pinning this whole custody claim on."

"I thought we weren't going to think about that. Or talk about it."

Silence, then "You're right. I'm sorry."

More silence.

"This isn't going to be easy, is it?" she said.

"No."

They walked through the parking lot, only the rhythm of their feet in harmony, and she searched desperately for something safe and neutral to say. When she couldn't find it, she decided that asking about Amy *ought* to be reasonably okay. "Does Amy spend a lot of time with your mother?"

"Since we found out about her illness, yes. She used to be in child-care for half my working hours and with Mom the rest, but child-care isn't safe for her now."

"Not safe?"

"Her resistance to infection is low. She shouldn't have too much exposure to other people. Specially kids. You know how they trade germs like baseball cards when they're that little."

"So she doesn't get to play with other kids?"

"Not right now. Her energy is pretty low these days, anyway. That's how we first suspected she was sick. She used to be so bright and busy, and then gradually she just..." He shook his head, couldn't finish.

"Adam—"

"Mmm?" He still couldn't speak.

She struggled to find something to say that would

help. Words were much safer than touch, but she couldn't find words, and touching him, which she so badly wanted to do, was getting more dangerous by the minute. Oh, but the whole idea of it was so natural and so right! Just to slip her arm around him and squeeze his firm, muscular body, tell him without words that she understood.

And without quite knowing how it had happened, she had done it. She'd slid her hand between his arm and his torso to find an immediate response from him, in the way his arm dropped around her shoulder and held her close.

So close. Amy's aunt and Amy's father. Already she didn't know who was supporting who. Maybe she was the one who needed him. She wanted to lean into his warm body and take its heat like nourishment. She wanted to run her hand down his back and learn the shape of his muscles and sinews and bones. She wanted to talk to him like a lover, tell him everything would be all right, *Amy* would be all right because she, Meg, was here with him and they'd each give the other the strength needed to get through anything that lay ahead, no matter how hard.

But that's impossible, she knew. That's not the way it is. I'm feeling this way...I guess we both are...because of what's going on. What we're sharing and what we're about to share...is so intense, but we're not lovers and we never will be. We're Amy's aunt and Amy's father, and the only thing we truly have in common is that we care about her.

And care for a child could make a man ruthless. The thought entered her mind as if whispered in her ear with a malign voice.

Adam felt Meg stiffen and had to fight the urge to

try and relax her with a more intimate caress. What exactly was happening here? How could he possibly let himself want this woman?

Trouble was, a healthy male didn't always have the control he needed in that department. Against all good sense, he'd wanted her from the word go, and the feeling wasn't going away. It was getting stronger.

If anything, she looked even better today in close-fitting casual dark pants and a thin, cream knit sweater than she'd looked in yesterday's neat, pretty suit. Her curves were more apparent, more touchable and, heaven help him, he was touching them now. She had been the one to initiate their contact, but he'd jumped right in there without so much as a second's thought about what it meant, and what he risked.

Predictable result. His skin crawled with need, and blood was pumping in places that weren't particularly comfortable. His heart was working overtime. And he wanted to explore—this warm curve here, where her hips flared gently outwards to her fabulously caress-able rear end. This nudging heaviness here, just above, which was the underside of her very female breast. This neat little row of knobs which were her backbone.

Her suddenly ramrod stiff backbone, matching her suddenly tightened shoulders and her suddenly lifted chin.

"How far is your car?" she said, pulling away as she spoke. The movement didn't surprise him. What-ever conclusion she'd so abruptly reached about what it meant for them to be touching like this, she'd acted on it straightaway.

"Right here," he answered, echoing her own crisp

tone. "Doctors' lot." He gestured at the dark green vehicle.

"Mine's two lots farther away. Maybe we should go separately. Meet at your parents' house."

"If you like." He wasn't going to force the issue. He needed her too much to argue about *anything*, even something as trivial as transport. "Can you find it? Mom and Dad's place isn't exactly inner-city."

"I have a map. Just give me the address."

"You don't need a map," he realized aloud. "Follow me, instead."

"I'd prefer to use the map."

"Stubborn." He couldn't help the observation.

"No," she retorted, "I just happen to like maps."

"You *like* maps?" Not something he'd ever heard a woman say before.

His scepticism must have shown. She gave a half-apologetic grin.

"Suit yourself," he told her, then unlocked his car and reached into the glove compartment to pull out a pen and a piece of scrap paper and scribbled down his parents' address.

Arriving first and parking out in the street to wait for her, Adam had no more than four minutes to wonder whether she'd gotten lost before she pulled up behind him in her small, blue two-door.

Remembering yesterday's suit, he concluded that she liked blue, and that she had pretty good taste. Blue suited her, even in cars. Then, when he eyed her dark gray and cream outfit once again, and took in the background of a bed of red and yellow tulips in his parents' front yard, he had to wonder if there was any color that *didn't* suit her. There was something about her coloring and the freshness of her skin...

Yet again, he pushed his awareness of her aside to deal with what really mattered.

Beth Callahan met them at the door. Adam had stayed the night here with Amy after his meeting and dinner with Meg yesterday, so his mother knew exactly what was going on. Both women seemed polite but a little wary when he made introductions, and Mom didn't waste any time before leading them inside and filling him in on Amy's morning. Normally, she'd have been much friendlier to any woman Adam introduced her to.

"She just woke up from a two-hour nap about ten minutes ago," Mom said. She's sitting in her crib playing right now. She seems cheerful, but still a little tired. She'll nap again for you later, I'm sure of it. If you don't mind, I'm going shopping for a while then I'll go over to Tom and Julie's to see the twins." His brother and sister-in-law, who'd gotten married last July.

"You're sitting for Julie?" he asked.

"No, Tom's gotten her to accept some paid help now, but I feel bad that I haven't seen them for two weeks. Babies grow so fast. They're three months old, already! But I've been so busy."

Busy with Amy.

She didn't say it, but Adam was getting concerned. Mom looked tired and stressed. She'd raised eight boys of her own—he himself was number three—and she'd earned some time to herself. She didn't need to be spending up to fourteen hours a day with her granddaughter as she'd done since Amy's leukemia was diagnosed. But whenever Adam so much as mentioned the word "nanny" Mom would practically put her hands over her ears.

"Great, Mom. Shop till you drop. I don't have to start work again until eight tonight."

"Then you're on *all* night, right?"

He shrugged. "It's okay. I'll catch some z's in the on-call room."

"If you're lucky. I married a doctor, remember? I know the drill."

She grabbed her purse, gave an uncertain smile at Meg and left at once, with a little eddy of awkwardness in her wake, swirling around the big and pleasantly shabby front hall of the sprawling Callahan family home.

The awkwardness didn't surprise Adam. Mom felt the way he ought to be feeling about Meg Jonas. The way he *did* feel, he corrected quickly, when he could forget the crazy physical pull between them. A mixture of wariness and need, in other words, with need winning hands down when he thought of Amy.

"Come and meet her," he said to Meg.

"She's upstairs?"

"Yes, in her crib, Mom said."

Neither of them needed to use Amy's name to know who they meant.

With his heart flipping back and forth in his chest like a pancake on a griddle, Adam led the way upstairs to show his little girl to the woman who might save her life...the same woman who was also planning to do her best to take Amy away from him.

Chapter Four

Amy was sitting up in her crib, wearing a purple playsuit dotted with tiny white flowers. She was surrounded by three or four plush toys that were already showing signs of being very well-loved.

Amy herself looked very well-loved, also, but she didn't show it quite the same way the plush toys did. Since Meg and Adam had both crept quietly into the room, the tiny girl didn't see them at first. She was watching the way the curtain at the far window billowed and sighed in the April breeze, briefly covering the face of an antique doll propped up on the toy shelf beneath. And Amy was laughing.

Meg thought that she had never heard such an utterly joyous sound. Did all little girls laugh like that? She hadn't had a lot of contact with small children.

"Peet-a-boo!" Amy said as the curtain drifted back into place. Then came another gurgling laugh as it billowed out once more. "'Ere's Dolly? 'Ere is she? Peet-a-boo! 'Ere she is!"

"There she is!" Adam echoed in the same triumphant tone, and Amy turned and saw him and her face lit up like a Christmas store on a December night. Oh, yes, she was loved!

"Daddy!" For several seconds she tried to pull herself up to stand, grabbing the vertical slats of her crib, but then her little legs folded beneath her again and she sat back down. "Daddy!" she repeated, just as happily, shrugging off her failure.

But Meg had tears in her eyes now, as she watched Adam cross the room to his daughter with his arms stretched out. That wasn't the clumsy collapse of a child who hadn't yet learnt to stand. It was the fatigue of muscles weakened by illness. Despite her happy, lively face, Amy looked ill. She was tiny, far smaller than most little girls of her age, and she had no hair. She was thin and pale, too, Meg saw, as Adam reached into the crib, picked her up and engulfed her in his arms.

There came the smacking sound of an exuberant kiss, followed by another gurgle and squeal of laughter. Ill as she was, this child's spirit was radiant and irrepressible.

For a moment, it seemed as if Adam had almost forgotten Meg's presence, but then he turned, still carrying his child, and the love-filled expression that glowed in his face changed.

"This is Amy," he said quietly. "Amy, this is…" He hesitated, and Meg was about to blurt eagerly, "I'm your aunt, Amy. Your auntie Meg," when she saw the hostile warning telegraphed by Adam's dark eyes.

"This is my friend Meg." He finished his sentence in a controlled tone.

"I'm so pleased to meet you, sweetheart!" Meg said, and was rewarded by a beaming smile and some gurgling words that she couldn't quite make out. Definitely not a simple "Hi," however. She fought to keep a lump from her throat. Cherie's daughter...

Then Adam added over Amy's head, "Is 'Meg' okay? Or would you prefer—"

"It'll have to be, won't it?" She didn't trouble to hide her anger, but then winced inwardly as Amy's eyes widened in alarm.

Great one, Meg, she scolded herself. This darling child is all set to think you're the original dragon lady, now!

Adam was wiser in the way he spoke. Amy's language skills were clearly quite advanced for her age, but she still responded more to tone than meaning, so his tone was cheerful and friendly as he challenged Meg, "Do you really think it'd be a good idea to tell her anything about your blood relationship at this stage?"

Meg smiled widely at him and adopted his own tactic for avoiding upsetting his child. "You're right," she said sweetly, "But why do I get the impression that you're going to use that as an excuse for keeping me at as much of a distance as possible? What is it you're so afraid of, Adam?"

"Obvious, isn't it? If you start to love her the way I do..." He didn't finish, and she knew she could have turned the little exchange into a victory for herself with one quick, clever line. But she didn't want to anymore. The truth, and what she really believed, were suddenly more important.

"Love doesn't have to be about possession, does it?" she asked. "Won't it be best if there's as much love as possible surrounding her, no matter who it comes from? You've already told me that her well-being is the only thing that counts right now, and you've convinced me. So can we...I don't know...take a walk in the park, or something? Just so I can spend some time with her, and you and I can both try our damnedest to stay off this subject?''

Adam didn't get a chance to answer straightaway. Amy had caught hold of a key word and was bouncing up and down in her daddy's arms. ''Park! Park! Go park! Backpack! Awwright!''

''My goodness! What did I say?'' Meg exclaimed in astonishment.

Adam laughed, his dark eyes crinkling at the corners as he tossed his head back. His laughter had the same joyous, alive quality as his daughter's. ''She loves the park,'' he explained, ''And she has a backpack that she rides in where she can see over my shoulders. She thinks it's the coolest thing that ever was.''

''Then let's do it,'' Meg urged. ''It's a gorgeous day.'' She hesitated. ''I mean, is it okay for her to be out?''

''It's fine,'' Adam answered. He grinned at Amy and tapped his finger on her tiny button of a nose. ''It's probably the best thing for her. Fresh air and sunshine.''

''Then, please, let's do it!'' she repeated.

''Sure...'' he said. As he turned back to her, Meg saw he hadn't quite let go of his reluctance. A moment later, he added more positively, ''Sure, why not?''

They left the house ten minutes later and walked west toward the park. Amy was riding high, head over

Adam's left shoulder and little legs dangling and bouncing as he strode along. He carried her as easily as he might have carried a rag doll, and both of them looked like they belonged together.

The two adults were treated to a running commentary on everything they passed as an arm stuck out and pointed. "Twee! Bird! Dod! Tar! Oh-oh, twut, oh-oh!" This last phrase came as a delivery van screeched its brakes to avoid a car, and the phrase was followed by an expressive "Whew!"

Meg laughed once more and said, "Oh, Adam, she's so adorable! And I can see where she gets her language skills from."

Adam had responded to each exclamation with a more detailed commentary of his own. "Yes, the tree is covered in blossom, isn't it? And that bird is such a pretty red. It's called a cardinal, honey." Meg hadn't realized it was possible to have such an involved conversation with a fourteen-month-old.

"I used to talk to her in the hospital a lot," Adam explained. "You have to be careful with preemies. Even talking to them can overstimulate them and tire them out, but she seemed to respond to my voice."

"Oh, of course she did!"

Who wouldn't? It was husky, male, musical, *sexy*...

"...and I used to feel like we were bonding, even when I wasn't allowed to touch her because she was so little."

"It must have been hard," Meg acknowledged stiffly.

She didn't want to think too much about what Adam had been through. All that did was strengthen the intuitive connection she felt to him. There was another side to this, she reminded herself. Cherie's side, which somehow she needed to understand much more deeply before she could think about trust or compromise.

They reached the park and began to meander along the cycle track which ran between stands of trees, and passed beds of blooming tulips and newly planted annuals and spreading, lush green grass. There were quite a few people out today, enjoying the magnificent sunshine. They passed joggers and cyclists and mothers with strollers. Adam told Meg about how he used the park as a kid with his brothers.

"We tried to improve the sledding hill one winter, by piling up the snow to make a jump at the bottom of it. Connor's and my idea. Didn't realize we were putting it right on top of the bike path, because the track was under the snow. Blocked it for weeks with this huge, six-foot high mound of snow which wouldn't melt until long after it was gone from the rest of the path. Didn't dare let on it was us when cyclists came by and cursed it as they detoured through the mud. Then there was the time one summer when we almost set fire to this stand of crab apple trees…"

"Who should I feel sorry for, I wonder," Meg teased. "Your mom, or your neighbors."

"Both, probably!" He grinned. "I mean, we weren't bad kids, there were just a lot of us, along with our friends. We were always having what seemed to us like such awesomely great ideas…"

They reached the crab apple trees. Then a woman, being towed along by a large dog on a very thick leash, was permitted by her pet to pause for a moment, right beside them. Her appreciative glance roved over the threesome, and she had time to comment to a still talkative Amy, "Gee, you look like your mom, don't you, honey?"

Seconds later, the dog had dragged her off again, and she never heard Meg's gasp of surprise, nor saw her wide-eyed look at Adam. "Like her mom," Meg said urgently, grabbing his arm. "Like Cherie! Does it mean that woman knew—"

"No, Meg. She meant you," Adam answered in a tight tone. A subtle tug pulled his warm, bare forearm away from her touch. "She thought Amy looked like you."

Meg's face burned. "Of course! Damn! How stupid of me!" Stupid, also, that she could still feel the texture of his skin as a memory imprinted on her fingers and her palm. The silky roughness of hair, the hardness of strong muscle beneath. "The three of us, walking in the park together just like a—"

"Family," he said, finishing it for her. "Dad, Mom and daughter. And she was right. Amy *does* look like you. More than she looks like Cherie. Or me, for that matter."

"Cherie wasn't a natural blonde."

"Tell me something I don't know!"

There was a short silence as they kept walking steadily, and Meg spent it wondering why the little incident had been so disturbing. The intrusion of Cherie, perhaps, reminding them both of a whole raft of unresolved issues.

"How did you meet, you and Cherie? Where did you meet?" she asked him out of the blue, then glanced sideways to find a profile that looked like it was etched in stone.

"In a shoe store," was all he said. Not exactly a detailed revelation.

"A shoe store? What kind of a—"

"Maybe you've never seen one before," he suggested sarcastically, cutting in. "It's a place where people go to buy shoes."

She ignored the biting humor. "Is it wrong of me to want to know a bit more?" she demanded. His stride had lengthened, and she had to quicken her own pace to keep up with him. "She was my sister. The two of you had a baby together."

He sighed. "No, it's not wrong," he said. "But it's not something I enjoy talking about. There've been times when I *didn't* look back on that meeting as the best thing that ever happened to me."

"But you do now?"

"I have a beautiful daughter." He reached back and touched the satin-smooth little hand that clutched his shoulder. "How could I possibly wish her out of existence?" A husky note darkened that sexy voice. "Yes, she's the best thing that ever happened to me. Cherie wasn't."

"*Tell* me about it, Adam!"

Tell her? Adam echoed inwardly. Yes, okay, he would tell her. She had the right to know.

"Okay," he answered aloud, then spent the next fifteen minutes as they walked, shaping his memories into words.

On his back, Amy had quietened and laid her head down, a warm weight on the pad of muscle between his neck and shoulder. He could tell she wasn't asleep, because every now and then she'd murmur a word or two, but she was already tired.

"Cherie wanted me to help her choose between two pairs of shoes..." was how he began it.

He remembered Cherie's face, laughing and flirty and outrageously beautiful. It was quite obvious which shoes she'd wanted him to select. Not the sensible navy pair. Instead, the scarlet Italian leather pumps with the impossible heels. The kind of shoes that kept orthopedists in business.

And he'd humored her, of course. Who wouldn't have? "The red ones."

It wasn't until she'd given them to the salesclerk to box up for her that she'd let him see the crutches she used.

"You can't wear shoes like that with crutches!"

But she'd laughed at his doctor's instinct to protect her...which had only made him want to protect her more. And she'd explained quite sensibly that she wouldn't be on crutches for much longer. Well, not *too* much longer. They were the legacy of a serious motorcycle accident when her ex-boyfriend—emphasis on the *ex*—had been drunk, and she'd really grown up as a result. She had been a model, but that wasn't important anymore. That was behind her.

She was twenty-four, she'd said, and ready to live in the real world. Impractical shoes, surely, were a harmless sin?

He'd asked her for coffee immediately. Looking back, it was the same joyously reckless impulse that had resulted in the snow jump at the foot of the sledding hill years ago. Innocent and well-meant, but leading to danger. He hadn't had this sort of impulse in a while.

Within a week things had gotten serious. Only trouble was, at least half of what she'd said that first day wasn't true. In hindsight, he'd learnt to divide the untruths into two categories. On one hand, the deliberate lies—like the fact that she was barely twenty, not twenty-four—and on the other hand, the things that Cherie herself had believed when she said them—like that she'd grown up and was ready to take life seriously, and like the times they'd slept together when she'd promised him it was a "safe time in my cycle." Hell, he was a doctor! He should have insisted to her that there was no such thing as a "safe time."

So she'd gotten pregnant, and for about a month after they'd done the test together and seen the positive result, things were great. She'd had her first prenatal appointment, and he'd gone along. They'd both seen the heartbeat and had had her due date confirmed by sonogram. Then she came off the crutches... started wearing those sassy red shoes...and the ex-boyfriend showed up, having dropped her cold after the accident, and wanted her back.

"That was when I suggested we get married," Adam told Meg.

Cherie had said yes, with an excited squeal. Adam had pep-talked himself for three days into believing it was the right thing. For their coming child's sake, maybe, if not for them. Then Cherie had run off twice. The first time on her own, the second time with the ex. That had lasted three months. She'd come back, her emotions all over the place, her pregnancy no longer a joy but something she spoke of as "ruining my figure, and my career."

She'd clung to Adam, but he'd known in his heart that she was using him. Someone to feed her properly, someone to get her to her prenatal appointments on time. And he'd understood by this time that what he'd felt for her had never truly been love. It was a mistake he wouldn't make again!

And then had come her premature labor, relentless and unstoppable, and Amy was born. Another erratic response from Cherie: "How can I invest myself in her emotionally when I don't know if she's going to live or die? I *have* to cut myself off!"

"But *you* made the investment, Adam," Meg said when he got to this point in the story. "That was incredibly...*courageous*," she suggested, trying the word out as if it was a garment she wasn't sure would fit. Adam watched her mouth, captivated against his will by the way it pouted like a juicy berry when she spoke with extra care like that.

"It wasn't courageous," he said, pulling his mind back to where it belonged. "I didn't have a choice. Some of the most important things in life are very simple, don't you think?"

"Yes, I do..."

"I just looked at my daughter and I loved her, and that was that."

There had been times when he'd envied Cherie her emotional detachment from Amy. She'd simply disappeared again, although according to the nurses in the Neonatal Intensive Care Unit, she called occasionally for news of her daughter. Adam himself hadn't heard from her. He'd assumed another reconciliation with the ex, but even now he didn't know for sure, and neither did Meg.

"I don't understand why she didn't tell us about *any* of this!" she said. "Not the accident when it happened, not the pregnancy, nothing about you at all."

"*Nothing* about me? That's not what you said yesterday!" he reminded her.

"I got it wrong. We assumed...*I* assumed until five minutes ago...that you were the ex, the one who'd crashed his motorcycle with Cherie riding on the back."

"No, that was a guy named Roy Ellis, but she used to call him Slash."

"That's right, and I can understand her not mentioning him, or the accident, until months and months later. She knew we'd be worried, or she was scared we'd yell at her. But why did she leave you out, when you were probably the best thing that could have happened to her?"

Adam shot a glance at Meg. Did she realize what she'd said? She did now, too late. She was biting her lip and her eyes had narrowed. It was a calculating look, and it shouldn't have made her look so damned pretty...and so damned vulnerable...but it did. Where was this planned custody claim headed if even the claimants' lawyer conceded he was a good, decent guy—someone who could put an erratic woman's life back on track, rather than derailing it?

But he forced himself to put aside any premature sense of victory. By mutual agreement, they weren't dealing with the custody thing yet, and anyhow, it wasn't as simple as just proving to Meg that he was a decent guy. He returned to the issue of Cherie.

"You know what she was like," he reminded Meg. "The good times with me were part of a fantasy for her, and just telling you and your dad casually over the phone probably wasn't part of the ending she had planned. She'd have had some scenario in her mind about springing wedding photos on you out of the blue, or showing up one day with a diamond-and-gold wedding band and a gorgeous baby girl all decked out in pink and ribbons.''

"She always liked to deliver her news in the most dramatic way possible,'' Meg agreed.

"Then before she could turn any of those scenarios into reality, she'd switched direction again.''

"Did she go back to Roy?''

"I guess so. Then she took Amy from the hospital, and I'm assuming Roy couldn't deal with having another man's baby around and that's why she dumped Amy at my parents' place during my brother's wedding.''

"Or maybe Roy wasn't involved at all,'' Meg suggested, a little frown tucking itself between her prettily arched brows. "It was about then, as we understand it, that she moved to New York and started modeling again. Maybe that didn't mesh with single motherhood for her. I think I'll call her agency and see if there's anything more they can tell me. At least now I know what questions to ask.''

"I guess it's important to you, isn't it?'' Adam said slowly. Every time Meg Jonas spoke, he found his understanding of her had grown by leaps and bounds. In some ways, it was a great feeling. In others, it made him deeply uncomfortable. "To get an exact fix on what was going on for her,'' he went on, trying to feel his way into what made Meg tick.

"I owe it to her,'' Meg replied. "There's such a lot I owe her that I can never give her now. I'm just trying to do what I still can...''

I'm doing it again, Meg realized as soon as she'd finished speaking.

Telling Adam Callahan everything, which was

about ten times more than she *should* be telling him. What was it about the man? Or did it say more about *her?* That, far from being the competent, cool-headed professional she needed to be, she was actually far too naive and trusting and far too easily pulled by her emotions.

They'd circled the park twice by this time, and little Amy had fallen asleep, her warm, satiny cheek pillowed on her daddy's broad shoulder. On bench seats, and on the warm grass, there were people eating lunch. When she glanced at her watch, Meg was shocked to find that it was after one o'clock.

Adam had seen the glance. "We should be getting back," he agreed. "I guess you'll stay for some lunch...?"

"No." Meg shook her head, calculating. She had a client coming to see her at two-thirty, which meant she could have accepted Adam's invitation—just. The timing also gave her the perfect excuse to leave, however.

"I didn't mean to sound reluctant," Adam said. "We'll fix a couple of sandwiches."

"No, really..."

"Hey," he cut in softly. "Things are going okay for the moment, aren't they? We've said a lot that needed to be said and finally we can relax a little. Shouldn't we maybe try to build on that?"

They'd stopped walking. Funny, in all the heat and revelation of what he'd told her about Cherie, they'd kept up a smart pace, as energetic and purposeful as mall walkers getting through their daily exercise. Suddenly, though, they were standing under a crab apple tree, bathed in a dappled pattern of shade and the sweet scent of spring, face-to-face and close enough to touch.

He was thinking of the bone marrow transplant and the connection that would be forged between them if that went ahead, Meg knew. But the whole subject scared her, and *not* just because it could take up to two hundred needle sticks, under general anesthetic, to remove the bone marrow that was needed, more than a pint of it.

No, it was the prospect of getting closer to Adam that really frightened her. Emotions were riding too high already. Hers, Patty's, Dad's, Adam's. The last thing she needed was to develop any sort of feeling for him.

"Not yet," she told him. "I'm…too uncomfortable with this."

"Why?"

"I…don't know."

But she did know, and so did he, she understood in a flash of insight. She could see the truth in the sudden, receptive stillness in his tanned face, and in the way his coffee-dark eyes had widened, while his lashes lowered over them like a screen. There was a connection between them. The oldest, most fundamental connection possible between a man and a woman.

It had nothing to do with Amy and her illness, nor Cherie and her past. Nothing to do with custody claims or cancer treatments. But it had everything to do with chemistry and physicality, despite the fact that it was the very opposite of what they both wanted.

He was the one to voice it aloud, and initiate the explosion that they were both waiting for.

"It's this, isn't it?" he murmured. Then he kissed her.

Meg Jonas was twenty-six years old and she'd been kissed before. She'd been kissed for longer. She'd been kissed more deeply. She'd been kissed in the dark and under the soft lighting of an expensive restaurant.

But she'd never been kissed like this, and had never responded like this. It was only a brush across her parted lips, under a spring-laden crab apple tree in broad daylight, but it was punctuated halfway through by the tiniest pause, just enough to let her feel the sweet-tasting warmth of his mouth and a faint whisper of breath as he reined in a groan of male need.

And though it was over in a second, it contained such a wealth of promise and possibility that, once again, she was frightened, the way she'd have been frightened—the way *any* sane person would be frightened!—at the sight of a lit match near a pile of explosives. Their bodies were dangerously, primitively attuned to one another, and under the circumstances it could only seem like one of Nature's jokes.

"And I never did think Nature had much of a sense of humor!" she muttered to herself, and had to suppress the need to wipe the back of her hand—her slightly shaky hand—across her mouth to get rid of that strange, fabulous, tingling sensation.

"Did you say something?" Adam growled. His eyes were fixed on her with such intensity, she felt like she was swimming in them.

On his back, Amy stirred and made a face in her sleep. Intrusive? No! A blessed reminder that the little girl was the lynch-pin between them, their source of conflict as well as the only thing they had in common.

"Nothing," Meg answered him. She tore her gaze away. "Not important. Look, I have to run. I have a client coming..." She looked at her watch again. "...soon, and I can't be late for that. So I really have to run."

Literally! As soon as they'd stumbled through the formalities, she was going to sprint out of this park like there was a wild animal in hot pursuit.

"Thanks for letting me meet Amy," she went on inadequately. "She's... Oh, darn it, Adam! She's a wonderful, darling little girl." Her voice began to fog. "And I want more than anything for...for..."

For a happy-ever-after in which Amy was well and Dad and Patty and Adam could *all* have what they wanted.

And me, came the insistent thought. There's what *I* want, too. What *is* that, I wonder? Somehow, I've forgotten...

As for Dad and Patty and Adam...

"Okay." He cut her off, as if her unexpected display of emotion was offensive. As if he didn't trust it or believe in it. "I'm glad you've met her, too. I'll let you know as soon as the test results are through."

"Thanks." She hesitated, then, "Look, what happened just now—"

"—was nothing," he agreed. "Crazy. And finished. I know. Forget about it. I have."

"Right. That's— Yes." Why couldn't she put together a coherent sentence?

"I'll let you know," he repeated. "Meanwhile, don't wait for me, since you're in a hurry."

"Okay," she nodded. "Thanks, Adam."

Turning from him and just, *only* just, managing to

stride rather than sprint, she found she couldn't even remember, what she was thanking him for. His permission to flee the scene like a thief in the night, perhaps? She didn't look back.

Chapter Five

It took eight days for the test results to come through. Eight agonizing days of waiting and uncertainty for Adam, and it didn't help at all that he was starting to get into the habit of enduring such days. The days after Amy's birth when they hadn't yet known if she would live. The days after Cherie took her from the hospital and he hadn't known where she was. The days after he'd mailed his letter to Cherie's father and had half expected it to come back with a purple, pointy hand stamped on it and the words "Return to sender."

Now, here he was with late April having turned to early May, and the trees in Meg's street bursting with fresh young leaves, standing in front of the door to her apartment with his finger still on the bell, listening to the peal of it die away inside.

He was carefully cradling inside himself the news he had to tell her, and he wasn't feeling quite the way he'd thought he would. For a start, she wasn't expecting him. He'd simply jumped into his car and raced over here, carried on the tidal wave of his emotion. Half an hour ago, that had felt right. It didn't anymore. He should have just phoned, kept his rush of feeling in check and treated this clinically.

Instead, here he was, heart pounding and adrenalin levels sky-high. He'd stopped very briefly on the way here from the hospital, on another impulse, to get—

Damn! He'd left it in the car! He turned and looked back down the brownstone steps and along the street to where he'd parked, then heard the click of the door, and Meg's voice behind him.

"Adam!"

"Meg, hi... Can I come in?"

"I wasn't expecting you," Meg said uselessly as she stood aside to let him through.

They both knew that, and *she* knew what it meant. He had some news for her. But whether it was good or bad, she couldn't yet tell. He was deliberately attempting to rein in what he felt, and yet he looked shell-shocked, as if reality hadn't quite hit.

She couldn't stand the suspense. Seven to ten days, they'd said at the hospital, so she'd been on tenterhooks since yesterday, both here and at her office, nearly jumping out of her skin each time the phone rang.

Since that day in the park, there had been no contact between them. She had wanted to call him. She'd even picked up the phone twice. But in the end she was too uncertain about it. There was too much potential for conflict to flare between them.

Leave it alone, she'd decided. Let *him* call, if there was something to say. So the weeklong wait was like the eye of a hurricane, still yet ominous, only an interlude before the maelstrom hit once again.

Now, she begged, "Don't keep me in suspense. Don't break it gently."

"It's the result we wanted, Meg," he said, and she could see how shaky he was. He seemed to fill her tiny entrance hall completely—physically with his impressive height and athletic shoulders, and emotionally with the sheer force of what he was feeling. "You're compatible. A better match than I'd dared to hope for. Given that, and the fact that we caught it pretty early, this type of cancer has a close to one-hundred percent rate of permanent cure, these days. Amy is going to live!"

"Oh, Adam, that's—"

"I know. I know!" He didn't even let her finish.

"Sit down," she begged again. He was prowling in her little hall like a caged beast, and she was conscious of every movement he made.

Without thinking she reached out both her hands to grab his arm and drag him through to her couch, and was shocked at the instant reaction of her senses when skin met skin. Over the past eight days, when she'd thought about that feather of a kiss in the park, she'd refused to consider that it meant anything. For heck's sake, it was a *moment*, a tiny, tiny moment, that was all, and when she saw him again, the feeling would be totally gone, evaporated like a morning mist.

Only it wasn't. It was back, and stronger than ever. More than just physical, too.

"Sit," she repeated as the backs of her legs bumped the smooth chintz seat of the couch. "And tell me what this means now."

But he shook his head and she dropped her hands from his arm. "First," he said, "I have something in the car. Mind if I—"

"Go ahead. Get it." It would be a relief to be alone again for a moment, to get her cool back.

He started for the door. At that moment, the phone rang, a distraction Meg didn't need right now. Still, it seemed easier to pick up rather than listen to the machine taking the call. She snatched it up and said a distracted, "Hello," still watching Adam as he headed across the room. He looked impatient and exultant. Exhausted, too, as if he'd kept going for the past few weeks through sheer willpower.

"Meg?" said her stepmother's voice at the other end of the line.

"Hi, Patty. I'm sorry I haven't called you back..."

Adam pricked up his ears at the sound of the name, the last he could hear of Meg's voice as he left her apartment again. Patty. The woman who was married to Meg and Cherie's father. The woman who wanted to become Amy's mother. The phone call seemed suspiciously timed, yet it had to be just a coincidence. Meg hadn't even known he was coming till she saw him at the front door. Logic told him his suspicion was totally groundless, but he couldn't make it go away.

Hell, he was a mess! A part of him was over the moon about the test results. It was like he'd crossed the finish line of a marathon or a car race. Maybe it was that comparison that had prompted his impulse to buy the bottle of champagne he'd accidentally left in the car. Here it was, sitting on the front seat, still chilled from the liquor store.

He unlocked the car, picked it up, then stopped.

Champagne? *Champagne?* It wasn't right. What was he thinking? Champagne was for celebrating weddings, graduations, awards, race victories. He hadn't crossed the finish line at all. The most important issue—Amy's life—was no longer in doubt, but there was still a long road ahead. The bone marrow transplant itself. Amy's gradual recovery and gaining of strength and health. And the little matter of Burt and Patty Jonas.

He put the champagne back on the seat and re-locked the car, reminding himself that the days were long gone when he'd go with a happy impulse the moment it occurred to him. He wasn't a kid anymore. At some point in the future, he vowed, he *would* celebrate—celebrate the life of a bright, healthy, beautiful little girl who belonged to *him.* He'd celebrate long and loud and hard.

But he wouldn't celebrate with Meg Jonas.

He'd left the door of her apartment slightly ajar, and as he approached it he could hear that she was still on the phone. Since she wasn't attempting to lower her voice he could hear her quite clearly…but maybe, he had to admit, he'd have tried eavesdropping even if it hadn't been so easy.

Because he'd caught Amy's name, and when it came to his daughter, he was prepared to toss the rule book on good manners right out the window.

"…take Amy illegally across the border to Canada, or something?" he heard, and his blood instantly chilled. He kept listening, not moving a muscle. There was a pause from Meg, then, "New Zealand? Gee, Patty, you don't do things by halves, do you?" Another pause. "Oh, of course I would, if that was the situation! But listen—"

Evidently, Patty didn't. There was another long pause before Meg spoke again.

"Okay. Okay, yes. You're right. I expect it would be quite easy."

Adam felt the strength go from his legs at the same time as one hand balled into a tight, aggressive fist. He grabbed the door handle for support as he swayed slightly, and it pulled shut with a gentle click, locking him out and locking in the sound of Meg's voice, so he had no hope of hearing the rest of what she said.

But what he *had* heard...

Had he heard it right? He knew he had.

"Take Amy illegally."

They'd go that far?

And he'd come so close to trusting Meg. It made him sick. If he'd had *any* sort of a choice, he'd have turned on his heel right there and only seen the woman again in family court, with his own lawyer by his side. But of course he had no choice. He still needed her, and more than ever now that she had, as he'd so desperately hoped, proved to be a compatible donor.

The ache in his hand told him how tightly his fist was still clenched. Using it, he hammered impatiently on the door and waited for Meg to come and open it.

"I'm sorry," she said at once.

"For what?" he growled, just to see what she would say.

Sorry that I'm planning to kidnap your daughter? That might be a nice start!

"That you got locked out. You could have left it ajar." She smiled easily, pulling his gaze automatically to those pretty lips of hers. "It's a pretty safe neighborhood. Did you get what you wanted from the car?''

"No, I…must have left it at work," he improvised. "It wasn't important."

Adam's whole manner had changed, coming on top of a difficult conversation with Patty, and Meg felt like she was standing on shifting sands. She'd been having difficult conversations with Patty almost every day for over a week, now, and it had taken all her skill with words to keep back the story of Amy's illness. Just now, with Adam's great news, she'd finally cracked and blurted out the truth, leaving Patty gasping.

"Oh, that poor, poor little girl! It makes me want her more than ever! She's going to need someone who can be with her full-time, not some career-obsessed ego-driven male who'll only squeeze a few hours a week for her into his schedule. My brother's a cosmetic surgeon, I know what it's like! Whereas I'd give up work completely to care for her… And to think what you're going to do for her to help her get well! Oh, I'm shaking!''

After a barrage of questions, Patty had gone on to talk wildly about the custody issue, and Meg was glad Adam had been safely out at his car, then standing on the far side of a locked door.

Now she suggested, "Uh, can I get you a drink? A coffee?''

"No, I won't stay," Adam said finally.

"No?" she questioned, taken aback. Something was wrong. Or was it just reaction setting in after the adrenalin effect of the good news had worn off? Whatever he was feeling, he was trying to hide it. The muscles in his square jaw were like knots.

"Don't we have things to talk about?" she pressed on.

"Someone from the hospital will call you," he answered in a stiff voice. "Amy's doctor. I'm expecting he'll want to schedule the procedure as soon as possible. How hard is it for you to clear your timetable?"

"Don't even think about that, Adam," she told him eagerly, determined to make him see that this was every bit as important to her as it was to him. Did he doubt that? Was that why he was holding back like this, and watching her like she was a lab rat in a science experiment, or something? "Whatever is best for Amy," she stressed once more, "I'll manage it."

"You'll take several days to recover. Is there someone who can take you home from the hospital and stay over with you for a couple of nights?"

"I'll think about it. Actually, I guess I'm hoping Dad and Patty will fly in."

His jaw tightened even more. "Yes, I expect they'll want to. But if you can't get anyone, I'll do it."

"No, Adam, really, that's not—"

"I'll do it," he insisted.

Somehow the words sounded more like a threat than a promise.

"Meg, are you awake?"

In her hospital bed, Meg tried to open her eyes. It wasn't easy. In fact it felt more like dragging back a heavy set of curtains than like simply raising two small stretches of fine skin. For the moment, she just couldn't get it to happen, and let them stay shut. Whoo-o... The entire world was dancing gently up and down. She was groggy, floppy, heavy-limbed, horribly dry-mouthed and sick to her stomach. And her hips and backside ached as if they'd been pummelled with stones.

Although it seemed like just a moment since she'd closed her eyes and started counting backward, as the anesthesiologist in the O.R. had told her to do, she had enough of her brain functioning to realize that the operation was over. More than a pint of marrow had been harvested from her hip bones. It felt like that, too!

"Meg?" said the voice again, the cruel, implacable voice that was asking the impossible of her. Open her eyes? Who was he kidding?

"No..." she managed. "Can't."

"I have some ice chips here."

Ah! Ice chips! That put the whole situation in a completely different light. Mentally, she swam upwards, out of the deep, dark waters of drug-induced sleep into a lighter, clearer state of wakefulness, and there was Adam. At first it looked as if he was swimming, too, floating like a mirage in the desert, familiar and wonderful and beckoning. Then he held the cup of ice chips to her lips and her vision steadied, and so did her mind.

"Thanks," she croaked, and felt the blessed relief of cold and moisture in her parched mouth.

"You okay?"

"Getting there."

"You were pretty nervous before."

"Two-hundred needles. Wouldn't *you* be?"

"And now?"

"Bruised. Tired."

"I'm really sorry your parents couldn't be here. You said your dad's company was fighting a hostile takeover?"

"That's right. He would still have come. I said no. But I didn't realize that would mean sticking you with this job." Adam had brought her to the hospital this morning, and would deliver her home again once she was discharged tomorrow. "My friend Joanne was out of town, and—"

"Don't talk," he ordered, gently firm. "More ice?"

"Please! But how's Amy? You should be with her, not me."

"I can't, unfortunately. I'm not allowed to."

"Oh, Adam, why not?" she croaked. She could tell from the way the short phrases came through gritted teeth that it wasn't something he was happy about. Had something gone wrong that he wasn't telling her?

"I'm getting a cold." He brought a tissue to his face as he spoke, and Meg saw now that he didn't look well. Before the procedure, she'd been too nervous to take the fact in, and he'd said nothing about it then. "Now, of all times!" he added. "And she isn't permitted to see anyone who has the slightest symptoms of an infection."

"But—"

"It could threaten her life, Meg. She has no resistance to illness at all until your bone marrow takes properly, and her blood count goes back up to where it should be. I'm anxious enough about the fact that I was with her yesterday before I felt this damned thing coming on, even though I was masked and gowned and thoroughly washed. Even if the unit staff would let me in over the next couple of days—and they won't!—I wouldn't risk it. Not for a second, when a sneeze could kill her. Mom's with her now, and she and Dad will take turns until I'm not infectious anymore.''

"Poor little girl!''

"She's very close to Mom. I'm telling myself she'll hardly notice I'm not there.''

"Telling yourself, but not believing it," she said gently, speaking her intuitive understanding aloud.

He nodded, but didn't say anything. His mouth was shut, making his lips thin to a tight line, and his eyes blazed with powerless anger that had no place to go. His hands were thrust deep into the pockets of his stone-colored pants, and his shoulders were hunched with tension.

Looking beyond her own aching, groggy body, Meg's heart went out to him and in that moment she knew, with absolute finality and the sense of a weight lifting from her shoulders, "I can't support Dad and Patty anymore. It would be wrong to even try and take Adam's daughter away from him, no matter how much we're hurting over Cherie and want a part of her in our lives through her child. She means the whole world to him. I won't tell Adam yet. He's not thinking beyond Amy's survival right now. And I need to talk to Dad and Patty first. Ultimately, it's their decision whether to proceed. But once I've talked to them—and surely they'll see that I'm right!—we'll be able to put all this conflict behind us.''

She didn't stop to analyze just why that possibility beckoned so enticingly, just added instead to her previous words, and really meant it, "Thanks, Adam.''

"For what?''

"For being here.''

"Don't thank me," he answered stiffly.

"Why not?"

"Because I'm the one that has to thank you. You've done something huge today, something incredibly generous. You've saved Amy's life."

"Oh, Adam, how could I *not?*"

"Still…thanks."

Adam didn't find it easy to say. Tipping the cup of ice chips to Meg's lips once more, and almost flinching as his thumb brushed her cheek, he felt nearly as dry in the mouth as she was. It wasn't pleasant to owe so much to someone whom logic told him to distrust. Even his hot, animal attraction to her had become a part of that distrust now. He hated the fact that his body burst into flames whenever they touched, that his eyes were drawn to her body as if he had a deep compulsion to learn every curve and texture of it off by heart.

And he *shouldn't* feel it! Not now! Not when she was lying here in front of him in a pale cotton hospital gown with no makeup on her face—damn, but she had gorgeous skin!—and dry white lips and blue shadows under her big eyes.

He brought a fresh tissue to his nose. If nothing else, getting sick should take away this pointless, dangerous clamoring of desire. Problem was, his brain and his body didn't seem to know how to talk to each other on the subject of Meg Jonas, and he didn't know how to restore the lines of communication.

The looming prospect of taking care of her for the next couple of days tortured him. It was bad enough that he couldn't be with Amy. It was almost *worse* that this meant being with Meg. She was going to be incredibly sore and sorry for herself for a good week, and the least he could do was be there for her. Make soup. Fluff pillows. Feed movies into her video machine. Say sympathetic things.

And keep an eye on her. Definitely that! He couldn't believe she'd actually be plotting to take Amy illegally while his daughter was still in the hospital and while Meg herself was so bruised she'd barely be able to walk. When he really thought about it, when he looked at her, he couldn't believe her capable of plotting at all.

Then he reminded himself about Cherie. Cherie had seemed so innocent and honest at first. Cherie had taken Amy. Cherie was Meg's sister. And he'd *heard* Meg talking about it on the phone just days ago!

Adam had never thought of himself as being a poor judge of character, but he had the evidence, and even with the evidence it didn't click into place in his mind. Instead, it went totally against his instincts. In the past ten minutes since she had opened her eyes, he'd seen Meg looking sleepy, sympathetic, thoughtful, grateful. He *hadn't* seen her looking devious or hostile or cold. Which meant...what? Did he trust instinct? Or evidence?

For the first time in his life, he truly didn't know.

She was watching him. Their focus met and got caught, tangled, like two rivers meeting. He wanted to look away and just couldn't. It was there again, and again they both knew it. Chemistry. Wasn't there a better name for it than that?

Desire? No, it wasn't only that, even though he could see the soft swell of her breasts quite clearly beneath the thin cotton of the hospital gown, and even though his fingers ached to touch the smooth, beautiful skin that flowed over her throat and collar bone and arms. Desire was only a small part of it, but he didn't know how to name all the other multicolored strands in what he felt.

And why was he torturing himself with the problem, anyhow? If he didn't think about it, maybe there was still a chance it would go away.

"They'll take you up to your room, soon," he told Meg. "You're only here in Recovery until they've checked that you've come out of the anesthetic properly. You'll have the IV for the rest of today, and you'll get pain relief and a liquid diet until tonight."

"Are you leaving?" Meg couldn't quite keep the regret out of her voice.

"Do you want me to stay?"

"No..." Yes! But she'd never admit it. Not when it made so little sense. That moment of connection just now... It kept happening, and she hated it. How could she think clearly about Amy, and Amy's future, when Adam kept getting in the way?

"I can," he offered.

"No, please!" She tried to sound firm. "Just hanging around? Please don't. I expect the pain relief's going to make me sleepy, anyhow."

"Probably," he agreed. "Okay, then, I'll go find a phone and call Mom in the isolation unit, see how Amy's doing." He wiped his nose, and she wanted to order him off to bed and take care of him, instead of having him take care of her.

"Let me know about her. That is, if I see you..."

"You'll see me," he answered. "Now get some rest, okay? You really need it."

And both of them were shocked when he leaned over and brushed her cheek lightly with the back of his hand.

* * *

He took her home the next morning. He'd been back twice the previous day, both times with good reports of Amy. She had received all of the bone marrow through the IV, and she was now receiving transfusions of blood and platelets to boost her immune system.

She was still weak following the radiation treatment that had completely destroyed her own diseased bone marrow, but she wasn't nauseous anymore, which was great, and her appetite had begun to pick up. Adam's mom had been able to explain that Daddy had a bad cold and couldn't come see her yet, and he'd talked to her on the phone. She hadn't said anything in reply, but she'd listened with a huge smile on her face, Mrs. Callahan said.

"And how about you? How was your night?" he asked Meg as they headed for the Emergency room. She was in a wheelchair, well-padded with pillows, and would wait in the Emergency room entrance for him while he brought his car round.

"Long!" she told him cheerfully. They had come out into the daylight now, to be greeted by gorgeous May sunshine. Meg had reached the conclusion sometime around two in the morning that hospitals definitely weren't her kind of place, and though she hurt, it was great to be going home.

"Painful," she added with a wince, as the wheelchair bumped to a halt. "Gee, it's hard to imagine that I'll ever be able to roll over again."

He laughed. "In a week you're going to care a lot more about the colors on your butt than how it feels."

"The colors?"

"You've got more bruises than you could count, remember? You're going to go blue and purple and green and yellow down there. You'll look like a Monet painting.''

''Great! Remind me not to go swimming till I've bought me a neck-to-knee bathing suit!''

It felt good to be laughing, and especially good to be laughing with him. It also felt good to know she'd *probably* never have to get stuck two hundred times with a needle in one day ever again...which made her think about Amy and all the pain she'd been through, while still so young. Less than fifteen months old, and she was already a heroine.

With a hero for a dad.

''I'll get the car,'' Adam said. ''It's in the doctor's lot, so it's not far.''

Meg watched him as he strode off to get his car. Just the way he walked told her that he was a fighter, with all the stamina needed for a long, slow battle, never a quitter. He'd been fighting for Amy for a long time already.

He pulled up at the curb in front of Meg two minutes later, and she saw that he'd thought ahead to cater for her comfort. The passenger seat was laid back and filled with soft pillows, and he had the door open for her before she'd even begun to get out of the wheelchair. He settled her into the car, leaning over her and putting an arm around her shoulder to help her get comfortable. The weight of his hand felt so right.

The hospital orderly, who'd pushed her this far, had nothing to do but return the wheelchair to where it belonged.

''Now, just remind me. How do I get to your place?'' Adam said as they drove off, and it was the start of a great day. A day in the full flowering of spring. A day when, at last, Meg started to see Adam relax a little as a phone call to the hospital as soon as they reached her apartment confirmed that Amy was still doing well. "Exceptionally well," her doctor had said.

Like her father, Amy was a fighter, too.

"Bed, or the couch?" Adam asked Meg when they entered her apartment.

"The couch." And don't even *think* about why that seems like the only safe choice, Meg Jonas!

He went through to her bedroom, anyway, and brought back pillows and a knitted blanket, then tucked her up on the chintz three-seater couch. Again, his hands felt as if they belonged around her body. Finally, he opened the drapes to let in a flood of sunshine and poured her a glass of iced tea. She drank it, then fell into a short doze, to be awoken by the return of pain as the effect of her pain pills wore off, and by the sound of her front door clicking shut behind Adam. He must have been back out to his car, and now he'd returned. With a picnic.

"Adam!"

"Gotta keep your strength up." He was unpacking everything as he spoke.

"For what?" she protested. "I'm not doing anything! Really, I'm not used to this."

"Not used to it?"

"To being an invalid."

"You've never been ill before?"

The food made a mountain on the coffee table in front of them, and when he'd finished unpacking, he sat down beside it, leaning forward and resting his forearms on his thighs.

"Horses have got nothing on me," she said, deliberately exaggerating. If he was going to look after her like this, she wasn't going to be a grumpy, complaining patient. "Is there another animal that's healthier than a horse? Because if there is, then I'm healthier than *that*."

"You don't look it." He raised his head to study her for a moment. His smile was curious and teasing, and did strange things to her insides...or was this just a side effect of the medication?

"I know," she answered him, in severe danger of forgetting what they were talking about. "Which is why I'm sometimes quite insistent on the subject! Dad used to want me to stay home from school sometimes when I was a child because I looked pale, and I'd have to tell him, Dad, I'm just not sick!"

"Are you kidding?" He was teasing her. "You could have gotten major mileage out of that pale skin. Did you actually want to go to school?"

"Not always," she admitted. "But I couldn't stand the way Dad would worry. He'd have some important meeting that he couldn't cancel, so he'd have to hire someone from an agency to come in and sit with me. He hated leaving me with someone he didn't know."

"No family in California?"

"We were here in Philadelphia until I was fourteen, actually," she told him. "Then Denver for four years. And even though I went to college in San Francisco when Dad was transferred there, it never quite felt like home. Dad's likely to get moved around again by his company at some point, so there was no good reason to make San Francisco a permanent base. That's why I came here to start my law practice. With all the good memories from my childhood, it seemed like the closest thing to where I belonged. But, no,

we had no family anywhere. None that counted, anyhow. My dad's parents both died about twenty years
ago. Dad's brother works in Europe. Mom's parents
are crazier than she ever was. I think they're in Alaska
now. They don't keep in touch. Neither does her
brother. Dad's always had a lot of great friends, but
they work. Not a situation where he could call up and
say, 'Can you babysit my little girl?' So basically,
when it really counted, Dad and I were on our own.''

"You must have been very close.''

"We still are,'' she said. "He's a great person, and
so is Patty. I'm so glad they found each other, because
it took a long time. Dad dated people on and off for
years after he and Mom were divorced, but nothing
ever clicked. Patty's divorced, too. No kids. After her
divorce she went back home to nurse her mother
through a long illness for over twelve years. Had a
hard time of it, too, until her mom finally passed
away—which was a blessing by then. Patty met Dad
three years ago when she started working for his company, and they've been married just under two years.
She's forty-four, ten years younger than Dad, and
they're so good together.''

"My parents are good together, too.'' Adam nodded. "Only they've been married over thirty-five
years. It's great to see, isn't it? Times when I doubt
the reality of love, doubt a whole lot of things, I look
at my parents and the whole picture clicks back into
focus.''

There was a pause. They'd both forgotten about the
picnic. A long paper-wrapped stick of French bread
sat there, surrounded by containers of salad and
wrapped packets of cold cuts and cheese. The sun was
streaming across from the window and falling across

the blanket that Adam had tucked around Meg's legs. The warmth and brightness of it soothed her throbbing bruises. She was thinking about what he'd just said.

"I know what you mean," she answered him softly, then looked at him.

He was still parked on the coffee table and the light was catching his face, emphasizing the fact that there were lines fanning out from the corners of his eyes and scoring down from his nose to the corners of his mouth—more lines, deeper lines, than a man should have at thirty-one. "You're a serious kind of a person, aren't you, Adam?" she added.

It was a gentle accusation, and she lifted her hand as she said it, and reached out with her forefinger to trace the lines she'd noticed. "Look at these. They don't come from laughing, do they?"

"Some of them do." He was quite still, letting her touch him the way a frightened colt might have done, permitting the contact but wary about it, not taking his eyes from her for a second. "Not as many as I'd like," he admitted, with a rueful grin. "Will you believe me if I say I used to laugh all the time as a kid?"

"I guess so." She took her finger away, but kept watching him, as wary as he was about what had started to happen between them.

"It's true," he said. "My brother Connor was usually the one who had the crazy ideas, like building the six-foot high snow jump at the bottom of the sledding hill, but I was the one who picked the best spot for it, and who was still sledding on it when it was three-quarters dark, and past dinner hour. I was the only kid left in the park, still yelling with happiness at the top of my lungs, even though my feet were soaked and half-frozen and my ears were red and I couldn't feel my fingers at all.''

''And did you yell with pain when the feeling came back?''

''Yes! But it was worth it!''

She laughed, then suddenly realized aloud. ''I think I saw you! It could have been you...''

''Saw me?''

''Yes! It just hit me, when you talked about yelling and red ears and that snow jump. It didn't click two weeks ago when you told me the story while we were walking in the park, but now the memory's come back. Dad loves walking in the snow, and we would always go find a new park to try when it was really beautiful out—you know, all sunny and sparkling and ice-cold? I missed that in California, and so did Dad. Anyhow, I remember we were out walking one day and talking about something, not taking a whole lot of notice of where we were going, and suddenly this kid, about fifteen years old, came flying over the top of a huge mound of snow that we hadn't even seen, riding some torn hunk of plastic—I think it was an old sand-box lid—that he apparently believed to be a sled, and missed me by about half an inch. Dad turned on him and practically yelled his head off. Yelled his *own* head off, I mean, not the kid's.''

''No, he practically yelled *my* head off, too,'' Adam said wryly.

''You mean it *was* you?''

''The description of my sled fits,'' he admitted. ''It was an old sand-box lid. And I remember being yelled at by some guy with this skinny ten-year-old—''

''Eleven-year-old, and not *that* skinny!''

"—with huge eyes, standing next to him. I believed him when he told me I'd almost hit her, even though I'd thought when it was happening that she was...you were...a tree. I'd gone a bit off course, you see, and I was coming pretty fast, so things were a blur," he explained, with a shame-faced grin. "When I realized you were human, I remember being surprised that you hadn't screamed."

"Screaming's not my style."

"I guess not. And then I did apologize, didn't I? I'm sure I did!"

"You did," she conceded. Nicely, if she remembered. Polite and sincere, but with head held high.

"I'll apologize again, if you like. You must have thought I was a total jerk."

"No, I thought you were pretty cute," she said softly.

Now, where had *that* come from? She hadn't thought about the incident in probably fifteen years, but all at once the memory was fresh again and she remembered she had smiled at the boy, very shyly, had been quite dazzled by the wide, white, awkward grin he gave in return, and had spent a good month or more, as her preteen hormones kicked in, wondering whether there was a chance they'd ever meet again.

They hadn't, of course. Until two weeks ago.

Chapter Six

Now the warmth in the air didn't just come from that glorious shaft of sunshine spreading across the couch where Meg lay. It came from something much less concrete.

"Crazy," Adam said, still grinning, and Meg nodded a little dizzily. She knew just what he meant. "I mean, those things must happen all the time," he went on. "When you think of the number of people you pass in the street each day. Stands to reason one or two of them will come into your life at some point and mean something, only mostly you never realize it. Never realize you've met them before. If I hadn't told you that story about the snow jump on the cycle track, and then talked about it again just now, we'd never have known we had a memory in common."

Just an ordinary memory. Nothing especially significant about it. But somehow it felt important. Somehow, it had changed their relationship. It was like...like... Trying to analyze the feeling, Meg pulled another childhood memory from deep within herself.

Vacationing with Dad in New Hampshire when she was about nine, the year after her parents' divorce. Swimming in the lake, she had gone out beyond her depth and gotten scared. Turning back for shore, she'd swum several yards then panicked and stretched her feet down, choking and spluttering as she swallowed the lake water. She had found, to her huge relief, smooth, safe rock beneath her soles, instead of the murky water-weed she'd been scared of, that tickled creepily against her toes.

Yes, that's what this was like. Finding a rock beneath her feet. And the rock was Adam, and the possibility of what they could build together.

"I think our lunch is getting cold," he said, opening the salads and unwrapping the cold cuts and cheese. He'd already brought plates and silverware, napkins and cups and soda from the kitchen, she saw. He must have done that while she was still asleep. That seemed like an hour ago.

"Cold?" She queried his comment without thinking. "But it's—"

"A joke," he pointed out patiently. "Not late night television material, maybe, but, hey, I'm working under difficult circumstances here!"

"Sorry, I was still thinking about—"

"I know. The sledding hill. Me, too. Hey, do you want your pain killers?"

"Yes, please!"

She winced. Even stretching forward to take the plate of food he'd served out for her was painful, rolling her onto a fresh set of bruises. She felt like she was bruised all the way inside. Was that even possible?

She gulped the tablets down with the soda and ate, while they both talked some more. A nice kind of talking. Lazy and quiet and casual. About childhood and memories and the odd things in life that turned out to be important. Around twenty minutes later, the medication kicked in and she felt the pain dulling again. Adam produced a movie he'd rented and put it in the video player for her.

"I'll be back later with some dinner," he promised. "Give me a key to let myself back in, in case you're asleep."

"You're not going to stay to watch this with me?" she said, then could have kicked herself, only she didn't need any *more* pain right now because she had sounded too much like a plaintive child who fears being left alone. "I've heard it's a great film," she added, purely to save face.

"It is," he answered. "I've seen it. But if you'd like me to stay..."

"Heavens, no! You've got far too many better things to do than stay and watch my bruises change color."

"I can't see your bruises," he pointed out.

"True. And neither can I. And I *don't* intend to peek under my skirt to take a look! They can change color without an audience, and I can watch this movie without an audience, too. Go, Adam."

He did, and she watched the movie, used the remote to rewind it and shut off the TV, then fell asleep again. As at lunch, she awoke to renewed aching and the sound of the key in the lock. This time he'd

brought hot food—Chinese from a nearby take-out—
and another movie.

"This one I *haven't* seen," he said. "Do you want
to take a shower and freshen up a bit while I set all
of this out?"

"Mmm! A shower!" she crooned. "Sounds like
bliss! I've been too dozy to even think of it."

"Need any help?"

"No!" she exclaimed, then added belatedly,
"...thanks. I can manage just fine."

It felt intimate enough just having him in her apartment, just *talking* with him the way they had today.
Having him help her in the shower went way beyond
any point their relationship would ever reach, she had
to remind herself.

"Did you see your parents?" she went on quickly.

"Just Dad. Mom was having a sleep in the parents'
room in the unit. She was up with Amy practically
all night. But Dad says Amy's doing great, really
bouncing back after the radiation treatment."

"He's a doctor, too, right?"

"Yes, so his opinion counts. And he's not a man
to show it, but I know he's been more worried about
her than anyone."

The shower felt like heaven, and the aromas of the
hot food smelled like heaven when Meg emerged.
From her bedroom, as she dressed, she could hear
Adam singing sketchily. It was a kids' song about a
baby whale and it had an upbeat rhythm and a jolly,
lilting melody. She had to smile. It was a pretty nice
sound. He probably played kids' music tapes to Amy
all the time.

She put on the loosest clothing she could find, a
baggy T-shirt which she sometimes used as a night-

dress, and a pair of old, stretched black leggings, then wandered back out to the living area, still listening to him. He stopped his absentminded singing as soon as he saw her.

"Feeling better?"

"Much!"

And she didn't dare tell him, "Keep going with the song. That was nice," in case he didn't even realize he'd been singing in the first place.

Adam had their meal already set out, along with plates and silverware. By the time she sat down on her pillowed couch once more, the previews at the start of the movie were already running. Evidently, conversation wasn't on the agenda for tonight. She wasn't sorry. The moments of connection they'd had today were still so fragile and tenuous. Maybe they'd only happened at all because she and Adam had both managed to steer clear of risky subjects.

Or maybe they'd happened because Meg herself no longer felt hostile to him. Her decision to do all she could to convince Dad and Patty not to pursue a custody claim had given her a new sense of peace. Yes, she still wanted to give Cherie's child as much as she could, but it was starting to seem very clear that the first and most important gift of all would be to leave Amy's relationship with her father strictly alone.

It was possible. They'd manage something. Vacation visits to California. Weekend access, when Dad and Patty could manage to fly in for a few days. It didn't have to be an all-or-nothing proposition. If they all worked together, they'd find a way.

As the opening credits for the movie began to roll, Adam spooned the hot food onto their plates and the ache around Meg's hip bones began to ease again.

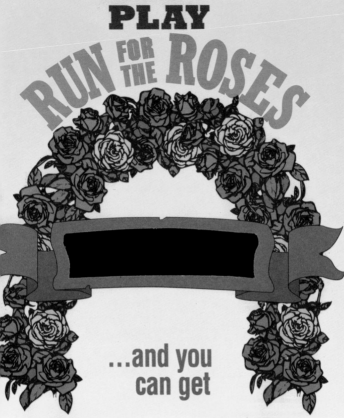

PLAY
RUN FOR THE ROSES

...and you can get

FREE BOOKS and a FREE GIFT!

Turn the page and let the race begin!

PLAY
RUN
FOR THE
ROSES

and get
THREE FREE GIFTS!
HOW TO PLAY:

1. With a coin, carefully scratch off the silver box at the right. Then check the claim chart
   see what we have for you — **2 FREE BOOKS** and a **FREE GIFT**—**ALL YOURS FRE**

2. Send back the card and you'll receive two brand-new Silhouette Romance® novels.
   These books have a cover price of $3.50 each in the U.S. and $3.99 each in Canada, b
   they are yours to keep absolutely free.

3. There's no catch. You're under no obligation to buy anything. We charge nothing —
   ZERO — for your first shipment. And you don't have to make any minimum number
   of purchases — not even one!

4. The fact is, thousands of readers enjoy receiving books by mail from the Silhouette
   Reader Service™. They enjoy the convenience of home delivery...they like getting the b
   new novels at discount prices, BEFORE they're available in stores... and they love thei
   Heart to Heart subscriber newsletter featuring author news, horoscopes, recipes, book
   reviews and much more!

5. We hope that after receiving your free books you'll want to remain a subscriber. But th
   choice is yours — to continue or cancel, any time at all! So why not take us up on ou
   invitation, with no risk of any kind. You'll be glad you did!

Visit us online at
www.eHarlequin.com

This surprise mystery gift
Could be yours **FREE** –
When you play
RUN for the ROSES

Scratch Here
See Claim Chart

YES! I have scratched off the silver box. Please send me the 2 FREE books and gift for which I qualify! I understand that I am under no obligation to purchase any books, as explained on the back and opposite page.

RUN for the ROSES	Claim Chart
👑 👑 👑	2 FREE BOOKS AND A MYSTERY GIFT!
👑 👑	1 FREE BOOK!
👑	TRY AGAIN!

NAME (PLEASE PRINT CLEARLY)

ADDRESS

APT.#   CITY

STATE/PROV.   ZIP/POSTAL CODE

315 SDL C246

215 SDL C242
(S-R-OS-05/00)

Offer limited to one per household and not valid to current
Silhouette Romance® subscribers. All orders subject to approval.

The Silhouette Reader Service™ — Here's how it works:

Accepting your 2 free books and gift places you under no obligation to buy anything. You may keep the books and gift and return the shipping statement marked "cancel." If you do not cancel, about a month later we'll send you 6 additional novels and bill you just $2.90 each in the U.S., or $3.25 each in Canada, plus 25¢ delivery per book and applicable taxes if any.* That's the complete price and — compared to cover prices of $3.50 each in the U.S. and $3.99 each in Canada — it's quite a bargain! You may cancel at any time, but if you choose to continue, every month we'll send you 6 more books, which you may either purchase at the discount price or return to us and cancel your subscription.

*Terms and prices subject to change without notice. Sales tax applicable in N.Y. Canadian residents will be charged applicable provincial taxes and GST.

If offer card is missing write to: Silhouette Reader Service, 3010 Walden Ave., P.O. Box 1867, Buffalo NY 14240-1867

BUSINESS REPLY MAIL

FIRST-CLASS MAIL   PERMIT NO. 717   BUFFALO, NY

POSTAGE WILL BE PAID BY ADDRESSEE

SILHOUETTE READER SERVICE
3010 WALDEN AVE
PO BOX 1867
BUFFALO NY 14240-9952

NO POSTAGE
NECESSARY
IF MAILED
IN THE
UNITED STATES

She felt a deeper sense of contentment than she could remember feeling in a long time…until about half an hour or so later.

It happened in the blink of an eye, when Adam got up to help himself to more Chinese. He tripped over the corner of the blanket, which had partially slipped to the floor, and fell on top of her, the weight of one hand pressing fully onto her bruised hip.

She shuddered with deep pain, and moaned aloud. Adam rolled off her as if he'd been stung. Meg rocked back and forth, almost nauseated by the waves of pain.

"Oh, hell! Meg!"

"It's all right," she gasped. "It's all right. It *will* be, in a minute."

"Swear at me, please!"

"Can't," she said, still shuddering as the pain slowly began to ebb.

He crouched down beside her and did the swearing on her behalf, berating himself so colorfully and at such length that eventually she had to laugh. Which would have been okay, except that he thought she was crying at first, and that set him off again.

"Just shoot me, okay?" he finally begged.

"Oh, Adam, I would," she promised in a melodramatic way. "I really would, only you forgot to tell me which video store you rented the movies from."

"Yeah, I guess," he agreed. "Justifiable homicide is one thing, but failing to return rented videos…now that's serious crime! Really, though! You're really not crying?"

She hesitated. Had he noticed that he was caressing her hip? Slowly. Gently. Rhythmically. It felt wonderful! Warm and sensual and tingly. What could she say to make him keep doing it?

"Some," she answered him. "A bit. What you're doing helps."

"What I'm—" He looked down blankly at his hand.

She was right. He hadn't noticed.

"Oh. Right," he said.

The hand stilled, a warm weight right at the top of her thigh, fitting perfectly against her shape. Then it slowly began to move again.

"And it helps, huh?" he questioned softly.

"Yeah," she nodded. "Seems to. If it's very slow. And gentle. And light."

"Like this?"

"Exactly like that."

"And here a bit, too?" he suggested, moving down to her thigh.

"Definitely there. Mmm...and there."

He'd traveled right up to the curve of her waist, now. She watched every inch of the hypnotic journey, and felt her nipples furl into tight buds at the very thought that his hand might move higher.

"What's happening, Meg?" he said huskily.

"Uh, I'm afraid I've...lost the plot, a bit."

He was leaning closer.

"I don't mean the movie."

She could feel his hair tickling against her forehead, and the sweet whisper of his breath on her cheek.

"Neither do I," she murmured against his warm mouth, and closed her eyes.

Their kiss went on for a long time. Not that she was counting the minutes. In fact, the whole concept of time no longer seemed to have much meaning, when compared to the salty taste of his lips and the way he said her name and the soft touch of his fingers on her neck and through her hair.

Nothing in her life had ever felt as right as this. It was right to have her arms around him, feeling the braided muscles in his back. It was right to brush her cheek against the unshaven roughness of his jaw. It was right to part her lips and explore him with her tongue, sensing his increasing need through every nerve ending.

When at last he slowly took his mouth away, fighting to control his breathing, she wasn't ready for it, and wrapped her arms around his neck to pull him back, begging him, "Don't stop, Adam," in a fuzzy purr of a voice.

It sounded wantonly seductive and she didn't even care. Her aching breasts were pressed against him. She could feel the throbbing tension of his arousal, and the quickened heaviness of his breathing. She wanted him, and he wanted her, and they both knew it, and somehow at the moment she couldn't think of any reason why there should be the slightest problem with any of that.

All of which meant that his next question didn't even make sense to her at first, as he pulled away again, more firmly this time, clenching his teeth for a tell-tale moment, and closing his eyes.

"How many of those pills have you taken, Meg?" He was looking at her intently now.

"Pills?" she repeated vaguely.

"The prescription pain killers."

"Oh, right." She frowned up at him, wishing he

would come close again. "Just like it said. The adult dose. One to two tablets, every four hours."

"And you took two every time?"

"Yes. I didn't think one would be enough."

"And I think two was just a little too much for someone of your build." He gave a brief smile. "Specially if you're the healthy type and not used to medication. How are you feeling at the moment?"

"All woozy. And the bruises don't hurt. It's nice. I don't seem to care about anything except what's happening right now."

"Which is a bit of a problem, if you think about it," he pointed out softly.

"It is?" She smiled at him. It was probably a pretty goofy sort of a smile, and it betrayed a lot, but she didn't care.

"Oh, Meg, for heaven's sake!" He sat back on the coffee table, his lean hands spread in a gesture of helplessness, and she was so startled at the abrupt change of mood that reality clicked back in again.

Kind of.

The movie was still burbling in the background. One character, a blind girl with no boyfriend, who had been almost too timid to leave her house the last time Meg looked, now appeared to be getting married. She had no idea how they met. They looked like a cute couple. Meg wished them every happiness.

The Chinese food containers sat in disarray on the table, like party guests who'd stayed too long. Meg debated her options with the leftovers.

A shadow from her grandparents' antique breakfront fell across the papered surface of the lounge-room wall and made a shape like a monster. Meg reflected that she'd always hated wallpaper and resolved to seek the landlord's permission to paint.

"Meg!"

"I'm sorry, I do feel a little strange."

"Have some water."

He poured her a glass and their fingers touched as he handed it over. It was instantly electric, and this time her mind really did clear and she knew what she needed to say. It would have been better to talk it over with Dad and Patty first, but there hadn't been a chance, and the timing just felt so right, now. Maybe it wouldn't feel so right any other time.

She drained the glass of water in four gulps, then said eagerly, "Adam, I know what you're thinking, what you're feeling, but you don't have to feel it anymore. I made a decision yesterday. I'm going to tell Dad and Patty that I don't think we should pursue any claim for custody of Amy."

"Excuse me?"

"I think you're right. Amy is yours and she should stay with you."

"This is quite a turn around, isn't it?" he responded on a growl, as wary as a cornered animal.

Meg could relate to the wariness. She was a lawyer and he was a doctor. Professionally, they both needed to be sure of all the facts, to see the whole picture clearly before they took action. Personally, it was no different. She hastened to explain.

"Of course Dad and Patty will still want to be involved in her life. I will, too, for that matter. She's all we have left of Cherie, and that's incredibly important to all of us. We can't let that go. We *have* to have Amy in our lives. But I'm convinced now that we don't have to do this through the court system."

"Oh, we don't…?"

"I'm hoping we can avoid any sort of formal, legal arrangement at all. If we could simply know that you're happy for us to have Amy occasionally. If she could stay with Dad and Patty in California for vacations. If they could come to Philadelphia for visits and take her out. If I could have her with me sometimes for a sleepover or an outing. That's all, Adam."

She finished and looked up at him with eager eyes and a smile on her face, expecting to see relief and warmth and happiness. *Wanting* to see it. Wanting so much to see the evidence in his strong body of a huge weight lifted from him. He hadn't always been weighed down like this, and he could be happy again. He deserved to be!

Those shoulders of his were so broad and capable, that face seemed so intelligent and caring and courageous, but a man…a single father…shouldn't have to go through what Adam had been through. It showed in him, it visibly weighed him down, and for some reason Meg had a growing emotional need to be the one to end the torture for him. She expected that what she'd said would end the torture right now.

She was wrong.

He was on his feet, on the far side of the coffee table. He wasn't smiling, and there was no sense that those shoulders of his had lifted. Instead, they gave the impression of having grown even broader, and his whole stance and the energy that radiated from him was hostile and almost menacing.

"You want to avoid any sort of legal involvement?" he growled. "Yes, I just bet you do! Because you *know* you have no hope in hell of winning. But let me tell you, Meg Jonas, there is no way on earth that I am *ever* leaving you or your father or your stepmother alone with my child!''

She felt like she'd been hit, and all the more so because Adam was reacting almost as if he'd done just that, despite the fact that, physically, he hadn't come near her. He'd gone white, his eyes were blazing, and he held his arms away from his sides as if his hands were tingling too hard to let them relax.

His reaction was totally incomprehensible to her, and all she could do was blurt out, ''Why?''

''Why? Because I don't trust you,'' he answered harshly. ''Not one inch. And if you thought that your attempted seduction just now was going to change that, then I'm sorry, honey, you were wrong. *Way* wrong! I admit, I was tempted.'' His voice dropped to a husky purr. ''And pretending you'd lost control because you were all woozy from the medication was a cute touch. Very cute. Cherie would have done it just the same. But it backfired, sweetheart. You might have gotten further if you *hadn't* tried to soften me up first.''

''Soften you *up?*'' She only just managed to find her voice, but it didn't matter. He ignored her, anyhow.

''And I said 'might.' Thinking about it, I doubt there's any way you could have handled this that would have gotten past me. Take that as consolation, if you like.''

He bent down and began to close the tops of the Chinese food containers, and she could only ask blankly, ''What are you doing?''

''Putting these away for you.''

And that was when her anger hit. ''Don't you dare!'' she yelled, straining her throat and making her bruises ache as she shifted. Suddenly, her head was pounding. "Don't you *dare* turn around and keep *helping* me after what you've just said! Get out. Just *leave,* okay? And don't bother to come back!"

He hesitated for a moment, and there was something in his face that, if she hadn't known better, she'd have thought made him look like he was being torn in two. Whatever it was, it didn't last long.

"Okay," he said. "I'm going. I'll be in touch."

There were a dozen things she could have said, and wanted to say. They all came crowding into her mind, jostling together and tangling her tongue so that nothing came out at all, and he didn't wait. He wasn't even looking at her anymore. He reached the door of her apartment in seconds, snapped back its two locks, opened it and left. It slammed behind him.

Meg slumped back on the couch. Two people in the movie were having an argument, but she no longer knew or cared who they were. Her head and her whole pelvic area throbbed dully. Purely for something to do, she picked up both remotes and pointed them at the TV and the video player, pressing the off button of one and the rewind button of the other. Silence fell, except for the whirr of the tape running backward.

For several minutes, she was numb with shock. His anger had come at her out of the blue like a runaway train, and she still didn't know why. The connection between them, strong and inevitable right from the beginning, had seemed tonight like it was about to flower fully. The way they'd talked today, the caring she'd seen in how he looked after her, those breathless, tingling moments before they had kissed when their little garnishes of humor had seemed like the only thing that stopped this whole room from exploding with the power of what their senses told them.

Even the homey feeling made by his snatches of singing as she came out of the shower. If he could sing like that, so easily and casually, as if even his voice belonged here, it proved she wasn't the only one feeling that there was something *right* about this

All that, and he'd accused her of *engineering* it? *Using* it? *Faking* it?

Aside from the fact that it wasn't true, it just didn't make any sense. Why hadn't he seen that she was offering peace and hope and happiness for all of them? How could he have thought it was part of some strategy?

"I don't trust you," he'd said, and after an hour of going over it all, again and again, she was left only with that.

"Talk about a poor judge of character," she said aloud to the empty room, and she wasn't talking about Adam's judgment. No, *she* was the one who'd gotten him so wrong. He wasn't honorable and open-minded and caring. He was paranoid and aggressive and controlling. Yes, say those words again, Meg. Paranoid. Aggressive. Controlling. Pretend that you mean them. Pretend they make you feel better. Don't admit, even to yourself, just why you're so disappointed that you were wrong about him.

And don't even *try* to think, yet, about what all of this will mean for Amy.

"Just go to bed, Meg," she finished on a sigh.

Adam was still shaking when he reached his apartment. Not yet able to relax enough to sit down, let alone do anything constructive with the remainder of the evening, he prowled uselessly around.

In the kitchen, he made himself a hot drink—his mother's old recipe for treating colds and flu. Boiling water, lemon juice, honey, powdered ginger and fresh garlic. It tasted absolutely disgusting, but he drank it, anyway.

He went into Amy's room, which had been his study until last year. It was still a source of almost painful pleasure to him that he had Amy back after those terrible months last spring and summer of not knowing where she was, and every time he went into this ultra-girl-child room, he gloried in the pink-and-cream color scheme as a celebration of what he had…and what he still feared losing.

Meg's apartment, so very different with its cooler, more adult tones, had cast a very similar spell of need over him today. Or at least, that was the only way he wanted to explain it. They'd had some great moments together. He could still feel the warm glow that had surrounded both of them when they'd discovered that silly childhood memory they shared.

His stomach was still replete with the evening meal he'd brought in for her, and there had been something so *nice,* just warm and familiar and *nice,* about setting out their meal while she was in the shower, then sitting there on the couch with her, eating and watching a movie, the way Tom and Julie did once their new twin girls were safely asleep, or the way his parents still did, even after thirty-six years.

Being a doctor, and knowing only the frantic, snatched relationships he'd had with a couple of fellow medical students, and then the doomed, histrionic liaison with Cherie, he hadn't had enough of those simple evenings at a woman's side in his adult life.

Then, when he'd stumbled and hurt Meg, he'd felt so powerlessly angry at himself, then so amazed to find she was actually able to *laugh* about it...

He'd forgotten all the complexities and impossibilities that already existed between them. The only thing he could think about was how good it felt to caress her hip, and how huge and beautiful her gray eyes were, especially when he saw them up close. And then, a moment later, how soft and warm her mouth felt against his own, how supple and tender her limbs were, pressed against him and wrapped around him, how perfect was the shape of her breasts, how fine and silken was the texture of her skin.

What was the real story with that medication of hers? He'd accused her of faking its effect, but maybe that was pure self-deception. If he was honest with himself, he knew there had been nothing one-sided about their kiss. *He'd* started it, and though she'd been the one to come back for more, he had been on fire with the need to give it to her.

He'd certainly been completely taken in at that point, and she'd been so adorable...or *seemed* so adorable...in her slight confusion. He had wanted to laugh and kiss her some more. A whole lot more! Not just her lips but her throat and her breasts and the tender skin at the crook of her elbows. And the bed in her room—queen-size, with a puffy blue and white down-filled comforter and about a hundred matching pillows, and the pajama dog she'd had since she was a kid still lolling on top—had kept coming into his mind, practically *begging* to be used. Likely the pajama dog wouldn't mind spending the night on the floor for once...

It was about then that she'd looked up at him, all eager and gabbling and happy—except he had to remind himself it was all an act—with her story about dropping the custody claim, and convincing her parents, and...just one teensy little proviso, here...as long as they could just *take Amy* sometimes, they could, all five of them, live happily ever after.

At her words, he'd remembered news stories he'd read, situations he'd encountered at the hospital...and Cherie.

Taking Amy.

He'd threatened her, and when he thought back on what he'd said, he wasn't sorry. He'd drawn a line in the sand, and now Meg knew where she and her parents stood, and what the boundaries were. They could pursue their custody claim if they liked, but they wouldn't win it. Or they could drop it and he'd let them see his daughter, but they wouldn't *ever* get her alone.

Most importantly, perhaps, the line in the sand was a boundary for himself. He was deeply grateful to Meg for what she'd done, what she'd put herself through for Amy's sake, but gratitude was as far as it went. He'd fight his attraction to her with everything he had, rather than let it blind him to the power Meg had to destroy the most vital thing in his life.

Adam's head was pounding now, and his throat was stinging again. He made himself another one of his mother's disgusting drinks and took some flu tablets at the same time for good measure, then called the hospital for another report and spoke to Mom.

After telling him that Amy had cried for him before

going to sleep, his mother asked, "How's Meg?" Before he could answer, she added, "I'm sorry I can't make it sound warmer, after what she's done, but the fact that she's interested in taking Amy—"

"There's a chance they may not proceed with the claim," he told her wearily.

"Oh, Adam, that's great! If she's seen sense at last—"

He cut her off. "Yes. So let's keep our fingers crossed, shall we?"

"Crossed? Mine are already in knots! But I won't keep you. Sleep well, Adam. You *will*, won't you? If this custody claim has really gone away? You let all of this consume you totally, and it's not good. You're hardly the same person you used to be."

"I am Mom," he told her wearily. "I will be, when all this is through. And I will sleep," he confirmed, hoping it was the truth.

He didn't burden Mom with the full story. Mom and Dad had shared so much of his pain over Amy. This new knowledge, at least, was a burden he would carry alone.

Chapter Seven

The light flooding into her apartment and the throbbing of her bruised body told Meg that it was morning, and that her pain medication had well and truly worn off during the night. It was her second night home from the hospital, and she'd spent all of yesterday alone. She'd tried calling her parents in San Francisco, but had only gotten their answering machine.

And she'd received a phone call from a nursing agency, saying that Dr. Adam Callahan had arranged to send someone over to care for her. She'd knocked that idea on the head at once, very politely but very firmly. She didn't need Adam himself *or* an agency nurse at his expense. That felt far too much as if he was trying to pay her off for what she'd done for Amy.

"As if he can't accept that I could possibly have done it out of love. Why?"

But something else was nudging at the edge of her

consciousness as well as bruises and morning light, and as she awoke fully, she realized it was the peal of the front doorbell. Adam, was her first instinctive thought. Come to apologize, explain, give her news of Amy, *something.*

She struggled to the door, trying to work out whether she was still angry at him, or hurt, or still just plain *confused,* and found it wasn't Adam at all, it was Dad and Patty and three suitcases. They both looked a little travel-stained and bleary-eyed.

"You're *here!*" Meg shrieked, pulling them into the apartment, then adding quickly, "No, don't hug me too hard! I hurt!"

"Poor darling!" Patty soothed. "Everything's all right, now. We took the red-eye and we've come to look after you."

Typically, she had started doing it already, crossing to the couch and plumping up the pillows which still lay there from yesterday. Watching the energy and care expressed through her slim, pretty hands, Meg thought, not for the first time, that it was such a pity chance had robbed Patty of motherhood.

"But I thought you couldn't get away, Dad," Meg said to her father. She had planned to try calling him again as soon as it was a respectable hour in San Francisco, and still couldn't quite believe that he was here.

"Yesterday was a nightmare. I couldn't even get to the phone all day, and by the time we got your messages on the machine it was too late, eastern time, to call back. The take-over went through," he answered. "It's a done deal, now, so there was no point in staying."

"Dad? Do you still have a job?"

"Don't know, yet," he answered cheerfully, running a hand through his hair. Fit and active, he didn't look fifty-four. If the newly organized company let him go, they'd be making a huge mistake. "Probably," he added. "But probably *not* in San Francisco."

"You'll have to move?"

"We don't mind if we do," Patty came in. She gave a loving glance toward her husband, and her golden-blond hair swung around her face. "Neither of us has strong ties there now. It would be an adventure to share. This new company has offices all over, including here in Philly. But we're not here to talk about that. You shouldn't be up and about, should you?"

"It's okay. I'm supposed to go by how I feel at this stage, and I'm getting better. Still sore, but bearable."

"And have you seen Amy, yet?"

"Not yet."

They talked about it while Patty fixed a hot breakfast—something she insisted on, even though Meg protested, "I haven't done enough physically to earn this, Patty! That bacon's going to go straight to my hips and take up permanent residence!"

"It needs to," Patty retorted. "You're too thin!"

For a woman who made accusations of that sort, Patty didn't eat a convincing amount herself that morning. "My stomach doesn't feel right," she admitted. "I guess the flight really tired me out."

Which made one decision easier for Meg. She didn't try and convince Dad and Patty to drop the custody claim that day. She would wait until they were fresher. They spent the time quietly and Meg hid behind Patty's insistence that she rest and not tire herself out with talk. Patty wouldn't even let her return the videos Adam had rented. Dad got directions to the video store instead.

"And we'll talk tomorrow," they all promised each other.

They weren't the only ones making plans for tomorrow. Adam called in the early afternoon to say he'd gotten the all clear to visit Amy the following day. "And you'll want to come, of course," he finished in a wooden tone.

"If I could," Meg agreed, just as cautiously.

"As for today, do you want me to come over?"

"No, thanks. My parents showed up on my front doorstep a few hours ago, and Patty's treating me like I've just delivered quads, or something. They're staying several days, and they'd like to see Amy themselves, as soon as it's possible."

"Not yet," he answered quickly. "I'm not taking that risk. I won't tire her out with more strangers, let alone ones who've just spent six hours with a whole plane full of Californian germs."

"It's okay, Adam," she answered, wondering why she felt such a need to have him know that she understood, after all he'd said to her two days ago. "Really it is! They'll understand. I don't know why you—"

She stopped. *Have such a problem believing that,* was what she'd started to say. Then she had remembered Dad and Patty, sitting in the same room. They didn't need to hear about what Adam had said the other night.

"We can extend our stay if we need to," Patty was saying eagerly in the background. "Can't we, Burt?"

But Meg's mind was elsewhere, and she didn't

catch her father's reply. Maybe they *did* need to hear the truth? She was torn. She was still convinced that dropping the custody claim on Amy was the right thing to do, even after what Adam had said, even if it really did mean never having the chance to have Amy to themselves for an outing or a vacation.

But could she argue to Dad and Patty in favor of dropping the claim if she hadn't told them what Adam had threatened? Exhausted by the emotional conflict within herself, she no longer knew where her loyalty lay, nor what was the right path to take.

"They wouldn't want to do anything to endanger Amy's well-being," she repeated.

"Of course they wouldn't," Adam said at the far end of the phone. There was a dangerous edge to the comment, and Meg had to think for a moment before she could pick up the thread of their conversation again. Wouldn't what? Oh, yes...

"They *wouldn't*," she insisted.

"Oh, I believe you," he answered. "Except that their definition of her well-being and my definition of it are poles apart, I'm starting to understand."

"Adam, damn you, that's not true!"

Behind her, Meg heard Patty's hiss of shock and cursed her own loose tongue. She'd never known a man who could trigger an unguarded emotional response from her so quickly, whether the emotion was anger or frustration or desire. Maybe that was because, until now, she'd never known a man like Adam.

He didn't reply to her outburst, just said in a controlled tone, "I'll come by tomorrow morning, around ten."

"Okay. Fine. Great," she answered, trying to sound breezy and cheerful.

Patty wasn't fooled, of course. The moment the phone was down, she had questions. "What isn't true? What was he saying? What haven't you been telling us, Meg? I'd started to get the idea from you that things were okay, that you were getting through to him. Or at least that he was starting to realize we care about Amy."

"He does... I think. I *was* getting through," she answered helplessly, then saw that she'd only increased Patty's anxiety.

Her golden-brown eyes were full of appeal beneath furrowed brows. "Meg, tell us!"

Meg slumped wearily onto the couch. "Not today, Patty," she begged. "Let me talk to him again first."

"But—"

"Let her be, Patty," Dad came in. "She needs to rest. And *we* need to trust her perception on all this. She's going to see Adam and Amy tomorrow."

Dad and Patty were out shopping in their rental car when Adam came by for Meg the next day. They hadn't said so, but Meg knew they'd deliberately arranged not to be here. Probably Dad's idea. Patty was too impetuous, and her emotions too near the surface to take the cautious approach, even when she knew that it was best.

"Pity. I wanted to meet them," was Adam's comment. It held no warmth. It was more like a threat, as if he wanted to assess them as enemies.

Maybe he's been this hostile all along, Meg realized, and any warmth I got from him was pure pretense. He was afraid if he didn't get me on his side,

I wouldn't go through with the bone marrow donation. Now that he's got what he wanted from me, he can let the mask drop.

It hurt. It *should* have made her spitting mad, bent on revenge and cold as a stone. But it didn't. Instead, it *hurt*. Physically. Deep inside. The way her bruises did. And it went against every sense she'd had when she was with him that there was a connection between them which they could both build on, to create something wonderful.

"You'll meet them soon," she promised him, as brief and cool as he was. "Let's go, shall we?"

"How're you feeling?"

"Not too bad. I'm still taking the pills, but even without them I think it would be hurting a lot less. Anyhow, I'm not thinking about me today. I...uh...appreciate your having me with you, Adam, when you haven't yet seen Amy yourself."

"You had a right to see her, after what you did for her. Don't think I'd forget that."

"And you'd feel that way even if I was the big, bad monster from the black lagoon, wouldn't you?" she retorted hotly, as if she'd been stung. "Letting me see Amy has nothing to do with how you feel about me as a person, as far as you're concerned. It's purely what you think you *owe* me, because of what I've done. Gee, I'm glad for Amy's sake that you didn't discover Count Dracula was a compatible donor!"

No response.

Pity. She wanted one—something hot and angry and blunt like her own words had been. It would have been a pleasure, actually, to sit here, both of them, in his car, yelling at each other before they'd even pulled out from the curb.

Instead, he stared ahead as he started the engine. Maybe he didn't even realize that she was glaring at his profile, wondering how there could be room inside her for such a mixed-up bag of feelings about one man, and wondering how that man could *live* with himself.

"Mom thinks we should tell Amy who you are today, and tell her about her new grandparents," he said as they drove.

"Oh, she does?" It gave her a small yet very welcome feeling of warmth to think that she might possibly have an ally in Beth Callahan. Although they'd only met for a few minutes over two weeks ago, in less than ideal circumstances, Meg had known that Mrs. Callahan was a woman she could easily grow to love.

"It won't mean much to her, of course," Adam went on. "Aunt and grandfather are just words. It's the relationship that counts. She loves Mom and Dad because she knows them, not because she's been told they're her grandparents."

"I realize that, Adam."

"Do you?"

"Yes! If you have a problem with what I said yesterday about Dad and Patty taking her for vacations, if that's what all this is about... Well, you don't need to. Of course they'd want her to get to know them and feel comfortable with them first. I'm not talking about just putting her on a plane."

"Right." The single word dropped into the air between them like a stone, then his mouth snapped shut again.

Meg seethed with frustration. Just what did she have to do to get through to this man? Physically, they seemed to slot together like two halves of a puzzle. On every other level, most of the time, they were speaking two different languages.

The issue dropped from her mind once they reached the hospital. The precautions they both had to go through before they could see Amy brought home to Meg just how real the danger still was.

"Watch how I wash my hands," Adam told her, before spending a full minute at the sink, soaping and lathering right up to his elbows, between his fingers and around his nails.

Meg had never thought of a man as having sexy hands before, but Adam did—lean, strong, smooth and dappled with just the right amount of hair. And the sexiness, like the soap, went right up to his elbows.

"Your turn," he finished, then stood aside and watched while she did it, reminding her, "Clean real well around your nails."

"Okay." Carefully, she copied him as closely as she could, then looked up at him. He was watching her as if he suspected she might deliberately leave some bits untouched. "Is that enough?"

"Just about. Give it a good rinse."

"How do I turn off the water?"

"Here." He stepped closer to hit the foot control, and his thigh brushed against her leg.

A minute later, he was tying her gown at the back, and showing her how to put on the disposable cap and shoe covers. Finally, he tied her mask. For him, none of it was intimate. He was a doctor and he'd done it hundreds of times. For her, each time he got close, each time she felt his fingers whisper at the back of her neck, or his hands nudge near her waist, she felt her body start to tingle and ache with its need to mold against his.

But when they finally went through the two pairs of double doors that led to the pediatric isolation unit, with all its sterile surfaces and intimidating medical technology, none of that was important anymore.

"Daddy! Daddy! Daddy!"

"Stay still, honey," Beth Callahan begged gently.

Amy still had an IV line snaking from her arm. She was propped up against a cool nest of white pillows, and was wearing her own stretchy little nightdress— pink with a Disney picture on the front.

"Hi... Hi, baby girl!" Adam said, and Meg could hear the choke and tremble of emotion in his voice, even through his mask. It made her want to stand right there beside him, holding him.

Instead, she hung back by the door of Amy's room, feeling out of place at this reunion, yet aching to have the right to claim a role in Amy's life, and Amy's father's.

"I'm so happy I can come and see you now!" Adam was saying. "I was so *mad* at that yucky cold! Daddy's here, now. Daddy's here, honey." He hugged her, then muttered, "Hell, I want to kiss her so bad! And *not* through a mask!"

"Only a couple more weeks, Adam, and she'll be home!" Beth said. "Just hold on to that."

"How much longer do I have to *hold on to* things, Mom?" he demanded, balling his fists in frustration. "What's coming next, I wonder?"

"Nothing!" she promised him. "After this, you'll

have a normal, healthy, happy little girl that we can all just enjoy and love and care for.''

"Dammit..." he muttered, and the comfortably rounded, gray-haired woman with the bright blue eyes pulled him close and kissed the papery cap on his head through her papery mask.

Meg turned to hide her tears. Where did she belong in all of this? They'd both forgotten she was even there. She understood that, and she didn't blame them for it, but it hurt anyway. Cherie's child. Her own flesh and blood. Her chance to build a better relationship than she'd ever been able to build with her sister.

But Beth Callahan had seen her now. "Meg," she said. "Don't stand back there! Come in!"

Her manner seemed much warmer than it had at their first brief meeting.

"Hi, Amy..." Meg came forward with the present she'd bought for Amy last week, a set of sturdy plastic farm animals, wrapped in bright paper.

Then she watched as Beth helped the little girl unwrap the gift, and it gave her a thrill inside to see Amy's face light up. But she felt stiff and awkward with the child. Didn't know what to say, and was all too conscious of Adam looking on. Talk about pressure! She knew she had to prove herself to him as someone who cared about Amy and could connect with her, but of course the more she thought about that, the harder it was to relax and let the new relationship come naturally.

Somehow, though, Beth Callahan seemed to understand. "It's so hard, isn't it?" she said. "This is such an artificial situation for a child, being in the same spot all day long. And she's tired of most of her toys, even the new ones we bought her for the hospital. Can Meg help you set out your new animals on the bed, honey?''

Amy shook her head. ''Me do.''

''Well, okay…'' Beth shrugged gently. ''I sing to her,'' she went on to Meg, ''And tell her stories, and we do finger rhymes. But 'Here's the church, here's the steeple' loses its edge after about ninety repetitions.''

''I bet,'' Meg agreed, laughing.

''That's Dr. Tanner,'' Adam said suddenly, craning to catch sight of a figure in blue scrubs and disposable mask, cap and gown walking through the unit. ''I'm going to talk to him now, Mom, in case I don't get another chance. I want to ask him…''

He was striding out of Amy's room as he spoke, and Meg didn't fully hear the rest of what he said. Judging by the stream of incomprehensible medical terms, she guessed she wasn't meant to. Subconsciously, she kept watching him as he crossed to the nurses' station. Dr. Tanner greeted him, then nodded and listened and nodded some more. Adam was obviously hitting him with a whole barrage of questions.

He had his back to Meg. Another time, she might have appreciated the sight of his long, strong legs, or smiled at the not-very-flattering cap over his thick, dark hair. Right now, all she could do was frown as the whole mess of her feelings about the man swamped her again.

Being with him and his mother and daughter was drawing her further and further into his life. And she was starting to realize just how happy she might have been to be there…except that he really seemed to hate her now.

''It's real hard being a doctor at a time like this,''

came Beth Callahan's voice, startling Meg and drawing her attention back to the bed.

"Is it?" she asked, speaking from her own sense of being out of place. "At least this is a familiar environment for him. I don't think he quite understood that for me it was all totally new."

"Yes, but he also knows every little thing that could go wrong here." Beth's warm blue eyes were steady and sympathetic, as if she'd read a surprising amount of what was going through Meg's mind. "I *know* he's staying up nights," she went on, "reading every book and article he can lay his hands on that covers her illness and her treatment. He's envisaging Amy with every rare side effect or setback that's ever been documented. I keep telling him, 'Just *look* at her. She's doing so well! Trust that, not some article about some case in Sweden or France six years ago. Amy isn't a statistic or a case study. She's herself!'"

"He's not very good at trusting, is he?" Meg said. She shifted position so she could look at him, and didn't make the effort to hide just how strongly she felt the need to understand him.

"Not at the moment," Beth said gently. "Have some patience."

"Have patience? When so much is at stake? I'm sorry, Beth, but it can't be helpful in working out what's best for Amy."

"Duice!" Amy contributed at this point.

"You want your juice, honey?" Beth clarified, and gave her the lidded "sippy cup."

Amy slurped the orange juice down with great relish. Beth took the cup away again and put it on the bedside cabinet.

"He takes things hard, my Adam," she said softly,

turning back to Meg. "He always has. It's because he really *lives,* and there are two sides to that particular coin. It means he's capable of great love and happiness and passion and success. I yearn to see those things in him some day, and I know I will. But it also means that when he suffers, it goes deep. And when he's angry..."

"But what I don't understand is why he's so angry at *me!*" Meg burst out, then gasped, appalled at what she'd said and who she'd said it to.

Beth looked shocked, also. "Is he? Angry at you? But I thought you and your parents had dropped any idea of claiming custody."

Honesty was the only possible response. "I want to," Meg said. "I no longer believe it would be right, now that I've seen Adam's relationship with Amy. But I haven't talked about it to my parents yet. They're very reasonable, caring people..." She ignored her memory of that phone conversation with Patty two weeks ago, when Patty hadn't been reasonable at all, and finished firmly, "I'm sure it won't be a problem."

"Still, I think that gives you your answer," Beth said. "Adam's not the type to relax about an issue like that until he's totally convinced that it's gone away. Meg, he just feels things too deeply! Remember that, and if you're starting to—"

She stopped, and Meg gave her a questioning look.

"No, never mind." Beth shook her head firmly, and shut her mouth more firmly still, but Meg was left with the feeling that Adam's mother understood far too much.

More than I do.

They were both startled, seconds later, at the sound of Amy laughing.

"Look at you!" Beth crooned. "What's so funny, little girl?"

But it was too hard for a fifteen-month-old to explain. She was grinning and pointing to Beth's mask and snapping her own mouth open and shut.

"Oh, it's my mask, when I talk?" Beth guessed. "When I shut my mouth quickly?"

Amy covered her mouth with her hand and started making a roaring sound. Meg came forward and sat in the second chair and pulled it closer. "Do we look like silly animals, do we, sweetheart?" she said eagerly. "That was a lovely roar you did just now. Were you being a lion?"

Amy shook her head.

"No? A bear, then! Let me see if I can make a good bear sound..."

"The curse of knowing too much," Steve Tanner said. "Really, Adam, shall I go through it again? She took the radiation treatment well. Her blood count is climbing fast. She's eating. All her signs are normal. You gotta relax, man, or *she'll* think she's not getting better, and you *know* how important attitude is, even in a kid as young as Amy."

"In short, I'm being a royal pain and I should get off your back?" Adam suggested to his professional colleague, Amy's doctor.

"In short, yes. Believe me, I understand. When my wife was pregnant I was a mess, and she was so darned healthy, she didn't even have morning sickness. So, please, buddy, let me get to the patients who actually *need* me, okay?"

"Okay," Adam laughed. It was a rusty sort of sound, as if his voice wasn't used to making it anymore.

He turned back to Amy's room as Steve headed out of the unit, and got a clear picture of Amy and Meg and his mother through the open doorway. He didn't intend to watch at first, but there was something captivating and heart-warming about the scene and he just kept looking as he quietly moved closer.

Dressed in her stiff, blue disposable cap and gown, Meg was making the strangest sounds, and Amy was mimicking them.

"Eeek! Eeek! Eeek!"

"Eeek! Eeek! Eeek!"

"There! A *great* mouse sound, Amy. Now, can you tell me again what sound a...let's see...a rooster makes?"

"'Ock-a-doo-oo-doo!"

"Beautiful!"

Amy repeated her rooster and Meg joined in with gusto. Coupled with her mask and cap, the bizarre noises were almost too much. Adam had to fight back a laugh.

"Now, how about a snake?"

"No..." Amy shook her head.

"A snake goes like this. Sssss!"

"Sssssssssss!" Amy repeated.

"Gee, how many sounds have we done now? Let's see, we did a bear and a lion and a wolf and a cat and a dog..." Meg counted them off on her fingers. "Eight! We've done eight different animal sounds."

Amy laughed and clapped her hands. Above her mask, Meg's cheeks were pink and her gray eyes sparkled with life. She really seemed to be enjoying herself, and enjoying Amy's responsiveness even more. Earlier, she'd been awkward, hadn't seemed to know what to say.

Adam had taken this as *proof*. Proof of exactly what, he didn't know, but he'd felt a cold sort of smugness and vindication. For heaven's sake, the woman didn't even *like* children, he had thought, willfully wild in his inner accusation. She didn't have the first clue about how to relate to them. Not the first clue! No wonder she was planning to carry out a kidnapping, or at least condone one! A child, to her, was about as feeling and real as a piece of jewelry. Precious and highly valued, maybe, but as a possession, not a soul.

He had dismissed his mother's sympathetic comments about it being hard to find ways to interact with Amy in the sterile hospital environment. Mom always saw the best in people, and anyhow she didn't know the full story.

Now, it was obvious that Meg *did* know how to connect with Amy, and she was doing it sincerely and enthusiastically and with no self-consciousness at all. Mom was laughing and joining in, too. The three of them just looked so right together. And though it didn't make any sense at all, he felt a warmth and softening inside, a sense of profound relief, as if he *wanted* Meg and Amy to love each other.

Dangerous to think like that. Remember, Adam! There weren't too many steps from thinking like that to saying, "Sure! Take her to the zoo for the afternoon while I'm at work." And if that brought a repetition of that horrible day a year ago when he'd finished a difficult session in pediatric outpatients only to find, when he had gone up to see her, that Amy was gone from the special care baby unit and the nurses were frantic…

If something like that happened again… Just how much more of this could a man take?

He stepped forward into Amy's room. "How about a frog, honey? Can you do a frog noise?" He was deliberately trying to pull Amy's focus away from Meg, and back to himself, like a toddler snatching back a toy, and it worked.

"Frebbit, frebbit, frebbit," she said.

"Perfect! And that's enough sounds for now, baby. You need to have your lunch and take a nap. I'd better take you home, Meg."

And he hardened his heart very deliberately when he saw disappointment replace the happy light in Meg's eyes. Let her realize right now! She had to do a heck of a lot more than make a few silly sounds to gain his trust.

Chapter Eight

"I would do it," Patty declared, checking her appearance in the mirror in Meg's room. It was almost time to leave for Dad and Patty's first visit to Amy. "If I thought it was the only way to protect a child from a really damaging situation."

"Patty, it's against the law!" Meg protested.

"There are higher laws than the ones you work with, Meg, honey. I'm sorry, but I believe that. When I read in the paper about a mother taking her child and changing its identity and hers, too... If she does it to protect that child from an abusive situation, then my heart is with the mother, it truly is!"

She burst into tears. Burt Jonas took her into his arms and soothed her. "You mustn't let this get to you so bad, Patty," he begged. "You've been all over the place lately, and you're not eating properly."

"And Adam's *not* an abusive parent," Meg came in. "Whatever else I could say about him, I'm sure of that."

She'd meant the comment as further reassurance, but Patty pricked up her ears and was on the attack. "What do you mean, 'whatever else'? There *is* something, then!"

"No, I only meant—"

"You're trying to get us to give up any thought of a custody claim. In fact, you've convinced your father and you've almost convinced me, and now we find out you *do* have reservations about him!"

"Not as a father."

"As what, then?"

"He's…"

She hesitated, and so many conflicting images of Adam Callahan flooded into her mind that she didn't know where to start. She took it slowly, staring at nothing but seeing *him*. Seeing him smiling and then scowling, fists clenched and then head thrown back in laughter. Seeing him when his eyes were soft and loving as he looked at his daughter, and when they glowed with the fire of the impossible attraction and intuitive connection that she herself felt, too, when they were together.

"He's had a hard road with Amy from the beginning," she began. "I've told you about that. The facts, anyway. Her premature birth. And when Cherie took her. Her illness, of course. And he's a passionate man, the kind who feels things very strongly. His mom said that to me, but I'd seen it…or sensed it…already for myself. And strong feelings are great when they're about something happy like, oh, the feel of the cold air on your face when you're sledding on a wintry day."

An image of him fifteen years ago in the park flashed into her mind, and she thought about reminding Dad of that memory, but decided against it, and went on, ''But it's not so easy when life gets tough. The pain runs deep. He has a strong sense of justice and honor, and he's a fighter, too.''

''You seem to have learnt a lot about him in a very short time. The way you talk about him,'' Patty said. ''You really seem to know him.''

''I—I guess I do. I've needed to, haven't I? To learn as much as I could about him, for Amy's sake, and ours.''

''Tell us, then.''

''You see, he's learnt, over the past couple of years, to be slow to trust, and we're reaping the results of that, now. It's going to take a while for him to trust how we feel about Amy. He's said to me there's no way he's going to let us see her unless he or his parents are there—''

''What?'' Burt exclaimed.

''And I'm torn,'' she confessed, ''between being so angry about that, and understanding exactly what demons of fear are driving him. For some people, love *is* about possession. How is he to know we're not like that?''

''How are we to know he isn't?'' Patty retorted.

''I can't answer that,'' Meg said. *Even for myself,* she added helplessly, without speaking the words aloud.

''It's time to go,'' Meg's father came in, with his usual common-sense approach. ''If this is about getting Adam Callahan to trust us, then being late for a first visit to our granddaughter isn't going to win us any points.''

This angle on the matter immediately blew Patty into such a panic that her husband once again had to calm her down, this time with a good laugh at her expense. She was able to join in, and the three of them arrived at the hospital in hopeful spirits and right on time.

It was a good visit. Amy looked even better today, and all her necessary measurements were still climbing as they should. Adam was alone with her when they first arrived, and the atmosphere was one of caution and restraint. Nobody yelled. Nobody betrayed any open hostility. Nobody challenged anything anybody else said.

Patty cried twice, and both times she was careful not to let Amy see. The mask and cap made this easier. With Adam, she walked on eggshells. "Thank you for letting us see her. You have no idea how much it means to us that there's still something of Burt's daughter left in our lives."

"I was happy to," he said carefully. "You're her grandparents, after all."

Patty could have brought up the custody and access issue at this point, but didn't. "She must be having such a hard time in here! How much longer before she can go home?"

"At least a week," Adam answered her. "Probably longer."

"You must be counting the hours."

"About two hundred of 'em," he agreed. "I'm glad the weather's warm. If this was happening in winter I'd be a lot more anxious, because of all the infections that go around then. When this little girl gets out of here, she's going to run in the sunshine, sleep as much as I can make her, and eat like a ten-year-old, aren't you sweetheart?"

Beth and Jim Callahan arrived, and Amy's nurse

reminded Adam that there was an informal but necessary limit on visitors in this unit.

"Meg and I will wait down in the cafeteria," Adam said. "If that's okay with you, Meg?"

"It's fine," she agreed, steeling herself for another onslaught of all the mixed emotions that hit her whenever she was alone with him.

Standing in a hospital elevator, with her hair still slightly flattened from the disposable cap she'd just discarded, she wasn't exactly ready for one of life's more earth-shattering revelations. Life, however, didn't seem to care. Meg got the revelation, anyhow.

I've fallen in love with him.

It was the only thing that made sense of everything she felt. The chemistry between them was something she'd accepted days ago. Maybe weeks. But chemistry on its own didn't count. She'd told herself the chemistry was an aberration, one of Nature's tricks, and she could live with it.

What she couldn't live with was everything else: the sense of knowing him, understanding him, to the point where she even understood the things about him that made her angry. The power he had over her moods, so that every evidence of his distrust and hostility hurt her to the core. If she hadn't cared, really cared, she couldn't possibly have hurt the way she did! And the way she was torn inside because, as matters stood, wanting what would make him happy, as he deserved to be, didn't necessarily mean wanting what was best for herself.

As usual, it all came down to Amy.

Now that she has healthy bone marrow, he probably wishes we'd all just vanish in a puff of smoke, she knew.

And she couldn't even hate him for it.

"Feel like a coffee?" he said.

"Yes, please!" Although not necessarily a coffee with him, the way she was feeling right now.

They left the elevator and headed for the cafeteria. "By the windows?" he suggested, running a hand back through his hair and rubbing his fingers around his forehead to get rid of the itchy feeling from the cap. "The isolation unit can get pretty claustrophobic after a while."

"I know." Meg nodded, helping herself to coffee from the machine, and hoping he wouldn't notice that her hands weren't quite steady. "Amy hasn't seen the sun for days, has she?"

"I'm itching to get her out in it," he agreed. "Before the weather gets too hot."

"Were you there in the unit last night?" Meg asked. It didn't seem possible that she could manage such a casual conversation. Was that really her own voice, sounding so normal, after what she'd just discovered about her feelings?

Adam had his coffee now, too, and they walked over to the windows. His stride was much longer and smoother than hers.

"All night," he answered. "I sat up with her. She was a little restless."

"Oh, Adam! You'll run yourself into the ground!"

"It'd take more than a couple of sleepless nights to do that," he retorted.

"Seriously, Amy needs you to be healthy. You don't want to get sick again and have to stay away."

"Have you been talking to my mother?" He glared at her from across the table where they'd just sat down.

"Your mother cares about you."

She wished she hadn't said it. It implied too strongly that *she* cared about him, too. But then she decided, why not? Why not *show* it a little? Simply that I care about him as a human being and as Amy's father. Surely that should do something to break down those walls he's put up?

"...and I understand how she feels," Meg went on. She leaned forward across the table and touched his hand, a brief, casual gesture that she immediately ended. For once, it was only about friendly support, not about chemistry. "And I understand how you feel, too, Adam. I know I can't prove that with words..."

Adam's pulse leapt wildly, simply from the effect of that tiny touch. It was all the more seductive *because* it was tiny, and he was convinced that she knew it. Any woman could come on strong, flaunt her body, play footsy under the table or engineer a long, hot kiss. It took someone clever and subtle and cool-headed to seduce a man using just one finger, as Meg had, so that his whole awareness was focused on that tiny patch of skin on the back of his hand, even while he felt the hypnotic power of it through his whole body.

He'd never been such an unwilling prisoner of his own senses. With Cherie? No, he'd had no reason to be unwilling at first, and later, as he'd come to understand who she truly was, he'd ceased to want her in that way. He didn't understand why it wasn't working like that with Meg. It almost seemed the opposite—that the more reasons he gave himself for distrusting her, the more powerful became their chemistry...and he really, *really* needed to find a better word for it!

She was sitting there, sipping her coffee and clearly trying to think of something safe to say. Strange how well he could read her. He could almost hear her ticking off the topics in her mind.

Finally, she put down her coffee and brought her hands up to her head, smiling wryly. "My hair's flat, isn't it?"

"No..."

It wasn't, anymore. It had bounced right back now that her cap had been off for a few minutes, but she fluffed it up, anyway, and Adam felt his groin begin to ache. It looked mussy now, and silky, and alive, and beautiful, all full of golden lights threaded in the dark strands, and he wanted to run his fingers through it and bury his face in it, and—

"So, have you been back to your office yet?" he asked desperately.

The look of relief on her face as she seized on the subject made him want to laugh out loud...and kiss her right on that bow-shaped mouth of hers even while she was talking.

"I went in for the whole morning," she said, speaking too fast. "Brought a pillow with me and sat on it. Glad I did. Go to the office, I mean, not bring the pillow. Well, I was glad about the pillow, too."

"I'm with you," he assured her solemnly. "I'm impressed that one pillow was enough."

She laughed, then admitted, "Well, it wasn't, quite. But the point is, I got a call from a client who..."

He hadn't expected to find it interesting, or to learn more about her through the subject of her work, but he did. For a start, she clearly wasn't the kind of shark who gave the profession a bad name.

"Don't you ever handle criminal cases? Or corporate clients?" he asked, suddenly curious to know more.

"Nope," she said cheerfully.

"How come?"

"I'm just not ambitious in that direction. I want to feel comfortable with my clients, and with the issues we're dealing with. For most people, buying a home is the biggest investment they'll ever make, and they get nervous about it. I'm there to reassure them that they have nothing to fear, that if there *is* something going on, I'll pick up on it. I caught a faked building engineer's report last week. Major structural damage to a suburban home that looked fine to the untrained eye, but it wasn't mentioned in the report at all."

"How did you find out?"

"There was something about the way the report was worded and set out that rang a few bells for me."

"Things like that must be rare, though. In between times..."

"In between times, I guess I just like sitting in a really nice office with a secretary out the front and the phone ringing, and papers and files stacked in neat piles on my desk, thinking to myself, 'This is mine!'" She laughed. "Is that a bad way to feel about a career?"

"A little possessive, perhaps," he teased, and he really hadn't meant it to be significant, but she reacted all the same.

Her cheeks flamed pink and her eyes widened and shone with sudden energy. She leaned forward and said eagerly, "Adam, I'm *not* a possessive person. I'm not! I *know* you're thinking about Amy..."

"I wasn't," he growled.

She ignored him. "...but believe me, my suggestion of taking her for vacations and outings *isn't* part of a master plan to steal her affection. Gain her affection, yes, but not steal it. Doesn't a child like Amy have enough love for all of us? I understand how hard it is for you to believe what I'm saying after what happened with Cherie. I want to prove it to you, and I know I can't, but—"

"Stop, Meg," Adam growled again.

Shifting in his seat, he looked both menacing and anguished, and if she hadn't been the cause of it, Meg knew, she would have wanted to come over to him, plant herself in his lap and kiss him until the warring feelings inside him went away.

"Don't you realize that every word you say digs you into a deeper hole?" he said. "Here are Mom and Dad coming over, and your parents. We're not going to talk about this now."

They didn't, although for both of them it took a heroic effort. Fortunately, the two sets of parents seemed happy to grab the conversational ball and run with it. Adam found that he couldn't make himself listen to all of it. He didn't want the four of them to get on like a house on fire, because then he'd have no one left on his side.

Apparently, the Jonases might not be staying in California, he gathered, and Patty, in particular, was embracing the possibility of change.

"In some ways, I'd enjoy spending a year out of the United States," she said. "Somewhere real exotic. Thailand or Venezuela. But of course I'd want to come back here and... Well, there's the question of spending time with Amy." She frowned, and went on quickly, "Have you travelled much, Adam?"

He gave her as friendly an answer as he could,

Mom and Dad chipped in with something about the extended vacation they planned to take soon, and it was all quite innocent... Except that he couldn't help thinking how well a year out of the country would dovetail with a plan to take Amy. Somewhere exotic. Somewhere that had no extradition treaty with the U.S.

And he couldn't help noticing that Meg had grown more alert when Patty was on that subject. Was she afraid her stepmother would say too much? Give away some half-made plan they were cooking up between the three of them?

He sat back in his chair and looked at the group gathered round the table. Five people, plus himself. Two sets of parents and their respective offspring. A stranger would assume that he and Meg were the linking factor. In a serious relationship and wanting their parents to meet.

He shut off the brief, treacherous thought that he'd *like* to be in that situation with Meg and focused on the truth. The link between all of them was Amy, and nothing about the group of them, or about the emotions running across the table, was as simple as it seemed. He had to force himself to appear relaxed, and Meg was doing the same...although he didn't examine too closely how he was so sure of this.

Bringing his attention back to the conversation again, he discovered that Dad had suggested dinner, and it looked like Burt and Patty were going to agree. He almost laughed at the sight of Meg rummaging around in her mental bag of polite excuses for one that fitted. She couldn't find anything, and apparently decided after a moment that she'd just have to grin and bear it.

Hell, he could *read* her! As if there was a clear glass window on that pretty forehead of hers that opened right into her thoughts, neatly typed. As if he had known her for years. It wasn't a relaxing feeling.

Dad had suggested a nearby steak house and everyone was getting up from the table now, scraping back their chairs. Mom found a private moment to say quietly to Adam, "I really don't think you have anything to fear from these people, Adam. They seem delightful and straightforward. And they're certainly not acting as if they still plan to proceed with a claim on Amy."

Well, they wouldn't, he wanted to tell her, if they're planning to take her illegally. They'd do everything possible to have us think they were "delightful" and "straightforward." He didn't say it, of course. He wasn't going to burden Mom with it, but the very fact of her relaxed confidence about the Jonases spooked him and ate big holes in the fragile new fabric of his trust.

It's what they *want,* he reminded himself.

Dinner went well until the end. Dad and Burt ate huge steaks and, once again, got on like a house on fire. Mom and Meg ate small steaks and talked about shopping. Patty played with a piece of chicken and looked as if she wanted to go to bed. The two older women went to the bathroom together at one stage, and came back looking like they'd just achieved world peace. Adam trusted it about as much as he'd have trusted a peace accord between Adolf Hitler and the tooth fairy.

He ordered salmon, ate it without tasting it, and didn't even realize he'd been ordered to make Meg eat dessert while the others went home until he heard Burt pull his rental car keys from his pocket and say, "Don't worry, I've already picked up the tab, but she needs to eat more, Adam, doesn't she? After losing all that bone marrow?"

"Can't hurt," he agreed, and only then understood that he'd be left alone with her again.

Their pretense with each other dropped as soon as the two sets of parents had gone.

"I'm sorry," Meg said at once. "I don't know why they couldn't see that we didn't want this."

"Maybe you did want it," he accused. "Maybe this is Phase B of softening me up. Will you give a report in the morning, I wonder, on how far you think you got? What do you think it's going to take? A kiss? Or will you have to go a little further? And has it occurred to you that I might just be playing along? Not fooled at all?"

It didn't sound particularly reasonable, but he was sick of sounding reasonable, sick of the pretense. He was ready to get this out into the open. She did a good job of looking horrified and confused. The waitress came with a perky inquiry about the dessert menu, and seemed a little bewildered when Meg waved her away. "I don't want dessert, thanks."

"Oh, but the other gentleman said—"

"I changed my mind... Adam, you're paranoid!" She attacked as soon as the waitress had gone.

"*Cut* it, Meg, just cut it!" he told her, his voice rasping with hostility. "It won't wash, okay? You see, I heard you talking to Patty on the phone two weeks ago about taking Amy illegally. Are you going to deny it and say I heard wrong?"

Evidently not.

"You *heard* that?" she echoed in disbelief, half rising to her feet in her indignation. Her cheeks were pink. Her gray eyes flashed fire. Her breasts heaved as she took in an angry breath. Even in the midst of it, he couldn't help thinking that she looked fantastic. So pretty. So intense. "You listened in? That was a private conversation!"

"I couldn't help it."

"Oh, really?"

"You hadn't bothered to lower your voice."

"I *thought* you were out at your car. And, anyway, the door was shut. I had to unlock it again to let you in. *How* did you hear?"

"I left it slightly ajar when I went to the car," he explained, growling the words as if he was the one who'd done wrong, although he didn't believe he was. "I heard you talking to Patty about Amy and, yes, I listened! Heck, she's my daughter and she was under threat and I didn't trust you, and I make no apology for that. I was right to feel that way! What I heard made me so sick I grabbed onto the door handle. Yes, I admit it, I actually went weak at the knees. You see I really *love* my daughter, Meg! Sometimes I honestly doubt that you know what the word means. And I dragged on the door and accidentally pulled it shut, so you had to unlock it for me. But I heard enough. Believe me, I heard enough!"

"You have *no idea* what you heard, Adam Callahan!" This time she was right up on her feet, hands splayed on the table, her whole body blazing at him.

"You're *still* doing it?"

"I am under no obligation whatsoever to clarify this matter—"

"Gee, you love your legalese, don't you?"

"—but I will, anyhow. Yes, Patty spoke to me on the phone that day about the possibility of taking Amy illegally. She hadn't met you at that stage, and I didn't yet know you well enough myself to be able to assure her one hundred percent that it was in Amy's best interests to stay with you. That's all she really wants for Amy, Adam. What's best for her. She told me that if she did believe Amy was in an abusive situation, she'd go to almost any lengths to save her from that. You see, she has so much love to give a child, and no child to give it to, and her emotions at the moment are pretty intense. I didn't try to stop her from talking that way because I knew she needed to. You must remember, Adam, what a shock this was to all of us. Cherie's child…and what we thought we knew about you…and Amy's illness…"

If she hadn't reached out to touch him at that moment, it might have been okay. He might have believed her, trusted her. But she did, covering his hand with hers then sliding it away again so that it felt like a deeply sensual caress, and as usual the effect on his senses was so devastating and immediate that it seemed impossible she wasn't aware of it, and impossible that it wasn't deliberate on her part.

"I don't believe you," he said, his voice as hard and cold as he could make it.

"You're paranoid, Adam," she answered, her eyes flashing.

Then she picked up her bag and left, and he let her go. Sprawling in his chair and wondering if he could have or should have handled it differently, he stayed at the steak house for another half hour and pacified the confused waitress by ordering a beer. He drank it without enjoyment.

* * *

"Paranoid!" Meg repeated to herself as she stood outside the steak house and waited for a cab to pass. "Aggressive!" she muttered as she hailed one and climbed in. "Controlling!" she decided, once she had given the driver her address.

They were the words she had used about him three days ago, and she didn't care that only the first one fitted. She needed to maintain her anger, and if that took a little willful inaccuracy, then so be it! "Paranoid" fitted to a T, and the other adjectives could go along for the ride.

She seethed until she reached her apartment, seethed a little more once she got inside, and only calmed down when she went through the day's mail and found a letter from one of the people who had worked at Cherie's old agency in New York.

It was a lead she'd been following up for over two weeks, now, and it had taken her a while to get hold of the woman, as she'd changed agencies shortly after Cherie's death, and had recently been on vacation. Finally, they'd talked on the phone the day before the bone marrow transplant, and Meg had been excited to learn that Cherie had written to Phoebe twice, while on a modeling assignment in Arizona.

"She was looking for a mentor, I think," the older woman had said on the phone. "She was trying so hard to stick to a direction she knew was good for her. Would you like to have the letters?"

"Oh, yes, please! Anything that might tell us more of what she was thinking and feeling, I'd be grateful for."

"I'll send them as soon as I get a chance."

And here they were, still in their slit open envelopes, accompanied by a short cover note. Still on edge after the scene with Adam, Meg made herself some hot tea and sat down to try and decipher the loopy, angled handwriting.

"Hi, Feebs!" the first one began. "Been doing some thinking and really wanted to get it down on paper and *tell* someone while it still makes sense..."

Each letter was four pages long, and Meg found herself wondering if Phoebe Cook had managed to read them thoroughly. There was a lot in there, much of it only assuming importance because of Amy, and because the living Cherie of the letters was now gone.

The most significant phrases seemed to leap off the page:

"...You probably don't know I have a daughter... I'm hoping to have her with me again soon...couldn't handle it for a while...her Dad has her temporarily...feel guilty 'cos I feel like I abandoned her, but as I said...and anyway, her Dad's a pretty good guy...not his fault that things didn't work out...so don't be surprised if I suddenly show up one day with a nanny and a little girl! Anyhow, there's that issue, and then the question of surgery. I'd really like to get my lips done..."

The second letter was dated just one day later. "Feeb, sorry to hit you again with another rave so soon, but things look different today...still not sure about Amy (that's my daughter)...I really love her, but..." Some scrawled curse words took up the rest of the line. "...in some ways I should have stayed with Adam. A guy *like* Adam, anyways... I *do* love her, and it'd be fun to have her with me, take her for walks in the park and all, but maybe it's not fair to Brett..." Meg hadn't heard this name before, but she could guess who it was—Cherie's man of the moment. "Another man's kid, blah, blah, blah. I'm so torn! When I get back to New York let's talk, tell me what you really think. The key question, what is best for the total Cherie Fontaine package?"

There was more, but it added nothing. Meg didn't know if Cherie and Phoebe had ever had their "talk." Phoebe hadn't mentioned it. Maybe the talk, like the rest of the second letter, had added nothing.

"Oh, Cherie," Meg said aloud to the empty room as she blinked back tears. "You sound about fifteen! So self-absorbed. You were still a kid."

And in all the vacillating about Amy, there hadn't been a word about how Adam might have felt at having his "temporary" life with his daughter come to a sudden end.

Meg took another look at what she'd said to him earlier tonight, inspected each word from all sides. Aggressive? Yes, but only when it came to going after what was best for Amy. Controlling? Only because her premature birth and her illness and Cherie's erratic ways had so badly threatened to undermine his control. Paranoid? Yes, and didn't he have every right to be?

Chapter Nine

Adam stretched then relaxed again in his rumpled bed. He felt good. It was six-thirty in the morning, but the room was bright and already warm. His chest was bare, and his lower half was covered in what passed for pajamas at the moment—an old pair of green hospital scrub pants he'd recently retired from their professional duties.

Lazily, he reviewed his options for the next few minutes. Take a shower? Appealing, but he was more than happy to postpone it. Make coffee? That could definitely wait. Grab the morning newspaper off the front doorstep and read it in bed? Nope.

Didn't take too much of an effort to decide. He was going to stay right here doing absolutely nothing and listening to what was, at the moment, his very favorite sound in the whole world.

"Baa-aa, 'at's a seep. Moo-oo, 'at's a tow. 'Oof-oof! 'At's a *dod!*"

In her pink-and-cream frilly bedroom on the other

side of the wall, Amy was playing. She'd been discharged from the hospital yesterday afternoon, and last night was her first precious night in her own bed. Adam had placed the set of plastic farm animals at the end of her crib when he'd crept in to check on her last night before going to bed himself, and he wasn't surprised that she was playing with them so happily now, and talking to herself about the animals and the sounds they made.

The set was the gift Meg had given Amy in the hospital, and it was her very favorite toy at the moment.

Adam and Amy both associated Meg with the repertoire of animal sounds, these days. At first, nearly two weeks ago now, Adam hadn't known what Amy meant when she'd asked, "Amal-yady? 'ere's amal-yady?"

Mom was the one to work it out. "Do you mean Meg, honey? The lady who made the animal sounds with you? The one who did the rooster going cock-a-doodle-do?"

"'Es! Amal-yady!"

"The animal lady's name is Meg, sweetheart. Can you say Meg?"

"Med."

The two of them, Meg and Amy, had made animal sounds every day since. They were up to seventeen of them. And now Amy was here, bringing images of Meg into Adam's apartment by making animal sounds in her crib at six-thirty in the morning. If he was honest with himself, he couldn't think of a nicer alarm clock.

It lasted another five minutes before there was a short silence, then a loud, "Daddy!"

"I'm here, sweetheart," he called back. "I'm coming."

He got out of bed at once, pulled on an old black T-shirt and went to her, ridiculously glad just to hear the word "Daddy" called with such confidence. It meant that Amy was happy to be home, that she *knew* it was home, and that she felt safe and wanted and loved here.

Reaching her room, he picked her up over the crib rails and held her close against his beating heart before he took her to her change table and put on a fresh diaper. Then they both sat on the floor, still in their nightclothes, and rediscovered all the toys they hadn't brought to the hospital, that she hadn't seen for over three weeks. It was eight o'clock before either of them wanted to think about breakfast.

The problem was, toys could take up the whole of a one-year-old's attention, but a grown man had room in his head for plenty of other thoughts besides. So, while he set up a wooden block barnyard for the plastic animals and made tall towers out of cardboard bricks for Amy to knock down, and did a silly puppet show for her with her three favorite plush toys, Adam thought about Meg.

There was a lot to think about. Since her stormy exit from the restaurant a week and a half ago, they'd seen each other every day at the hospital, which surely ought to mean that their relationship was developing in some easily discernible direction. Heck, the options were limited! As you got to know a person better, you either liked them more, or you liked them less. You either developed a friendship, or you began to treat each other with the distant wariness of cats. Occasionally, you found that you really couldn't stand a person, and that the feeling was mutual, and you avoided them wherever possible.

What you *didn't* do was hang fire like Adam was doing. He'd begun to feel that Meg Jonas had been a part of his life for a very long time. He couldn't remember how it felt not to know her. They talked. They laughed a surprising amount. They even ate together, at the hospital cafeteria, once or twice.

What allowed any of this to happen in the first place, was the apologies they'd each muttered and stumbled their way through the day after the storm at the restaurant. Again, though, they were strangely unsatisfying apologies, ones that went nowhere.

"I shouldn't have used the word paranoid. It's too negative. Too loaded," Meg had said.

"And I shouldn't have attacked like I did, when, as you pointed out, I hadn't heard the whole conversation," he had offered in reply.

Thinking about it now—whack! Another cardboard tower went flying and Amy laughed wildly—he realized that neither apology had really covered all the necessary territory.

He hadn't said, "I apologize for not having trusted you, and I trust you now," and *she* hadn't said, "I apologize for not having been able to see how huge this is for you, and I see it now."

So, ultimately, nothing was resolved. Maybe that was why, every time he thought about Meg and every time he was with her, he ached. Yes, *ached,* even when he was smiling at something she'd said to Amy, or agreeing with one of her quietly clever insights about life, or unconsciously noting the way the light caught her hair and brought out golden threads in the rich dark brown, or the way the fabric of her clothing molded against her very female figure.

Oh, yes, he definitely ached then!

For breakfast, he made them both bacon, scrambled eggs, hash browns, toast and orange juice as well as sliced banana for Amy, and coffee for himself. She ate enough of it to please even the most fearful part of him—the part which still dominated his being for much of the time—and then "helped" him clean up the kitchen. After he'd changed her entire outfit, mopped the floor twice and squeezed out four wet dish towels, it was almost ten o'clock.

The phone rang, and it was his mother. "About the party tomorrow..." she began.

"It's not a party, Mom," he cut in. He didn't like the word in this situation, not one bit. Could they really afford to be celebrating at this stage? He went on firmly, "Amy's not strong enough for something like that yet, although she ate brilliantly just now."

"The party's not just for Amy, Adam," Mom said. "It's for all of us. You're right about her strength. She'll probably be happy to toddle around the garden for a while before everybody gets here, and we can bring her playpen outside, and then the fresh air will tire her and she'll take a big long nap. But the rest of us need a party. Your dad and I do! You most definitely do. And I was wondering... At least, I presume you've invited Meg?"

"I mentioned it," he answered reluctantly. He didn't like the easy, warm way in which Mom said Meg's name.

There was a short silence at the other end of the line. "I guess that'll have to do. And what about her parents?"

"They've been back in California for over a week, Mom, you know that."

"No, they're flying in again today. I got a call from Patty."

"Gee, are you two best friends, or something?" he said sourly, all his distrust washing over him again.

"They're your daughter's grandparents. Which means they're family, Adam."

He ignored this, since he couldn't feel that way, and attacked on a different front, instead. "And what did you mean, just now, that'll have to do?"

"It's not important," she replied breezily.

He knew she was lying. "Mom, can you at least do me the courtesy of being *honest?*"

Ten minutes later, after telling him he was an idiot in about fifty different ways, Beth Callahan finished darkly, "And that's only *half* of it! I'll save the rest for another day."

When Adam put the phone down, his ears were ringing, his head hurt, and he knew he had a lot to chew over.

"Just my luck to fall in love with the most difficult man I've ever met!" Meg muttered to herself.

She poured herself a big plastic cup of soda and took some gulps, pretending it was all she cared about. Then she caught Adam looking in her direction again, with his usual black frown. They hadn't spoken to each other since she'd arrived at the Callahans' some minutes ago.

Standing in the middle of the sprawling garden, between a huge pine tree and a newly leafed-out maple, he was surrounded by a cluster of about four people. He stood taller than all of them. His hands were pushed deep into the pockets of his casual navy shorts and his skin looked tanned against the contrast of a white T-shirt.

She would have said he was totally absorbed in talking with everyone, and enjoying himself, too, judging by the way he was laughing, except for these glowering looks that kept coming her way. So why didn't he greet her?

She wanted to talk to him, in particular, because she had two pieces of news to tell, and the fact that she wasn't quite sure how he'd take either of them didn't make his ignoring her any easier.

Beth was the hostess here today, welcoming everyone through to the large rear yard while Jim got the barbecue fired up. Judging by the pile of steaks and burgers and hot dogs waiting to be cooked, they were expecting about sixty people at this so-called "very low-key, casual drop-by barbecue to celebrate Amy coming home."

But when there were eight kids in the family, all of them grown or nearly so, and when both parents came from large families also, sixty people probably didn't seem like a big deal.

And apparently, Adam was glad about the growing crowd. He seemed to be using every aunt or cousin or brother he could find as a good excuse not to come over and speak to Meg. He'd just grabbed someone else—a young girl of about twenty—and drawn her into the group, though the big hug he gave her looked pretty stiff and forced, if Meg was any judge.

"I don't care," she muttered again. "Really, I can't stand the man! It's a huge nuisance that I happen to be in love with him at the same time!"

A nuisance, but an education. She was getting first-hand knowledge of just how contrary a human being could be. It was a humbling experience, since she'd always considered herself a very rational person in the past.

Speaking of which, what might a rational person do in this situation? She considered the matter for half a minute, then went over to Jim Callahan at the barbecue. "Need any help?"

She liked Adam's dad almost as much as she liked his mom—liked his dry sense of humor, his twinkling brown eyes...and all the little ways in which he reminded her of Adam.

He looked at her in surprise. "Meg! I'm grateful for the offer, but can't you find something more fun to do?"

"Helping is fun, at a big family gathering like this," she insisted, meaning it. "Shall I start the steaks?"

"Sure. I think the charcoal is hot enough." He put a piece of steak onto the grill and it hissed fiercely. "Whoa! Maybe too hot!" Then he added, thoughtfully, with a quick glance in her direction, "I guess you don't know too many of this tribe, do you?"

"Amy's the one I know best," Meg said, deliberately overlooking the question of Amy's dad, "And Beth says she's asleep."

"Yep, we're celebrating without the guest of honor, but this is really for Adam more than anyone."

"And the two of you, I expect," Meg said, setting the steaks out on the grill. "I've heard people say they worry twice as much about their kids once they grow up than they ever had to worry about them when they were little."

"I heard that, too, when our kids were little and I

thought, 'Not possible!' These days, I'm starting to think there's something in it," Jim said. Then he ticked off the four eldest of his eight children on his fingers. "We've got Patrick, who refuses to admit that marriage to the right kind of woman would be the best thing that could possibly happen to him. We've got Connor, who likes to experiment with new ways of hurting himself while pretending it's called 'extreme sport.' Every time he heads up to the Adirondacks for some skiing or wind-surfing my chest aches from holding my breath."

Meg laughed.

Jim went on, "Then we've got Tom. Well, Tom's doing great now that he's married to Julie and they've got the twins, but it wasn't smooth sailing back there for a while."

Meg knew the story by this time. Julie had started out as a surrogate mother for her cousin Loretta, not realizing that Loretta's ex-husband Tom knew nothing about Loretta's scheming plan to win him back, for the sake of his newly gained wealth. It had taken Loretta's death to reveal the truth. Then Tom and Julie had embarked on a paper marriage because of Julie's pregnancy, and this had lasted for several difficult months before it turned into the real thing, shortly before the birth of their two baby girls.

"And then there's Adam," Meg cut in.

"And then there's Adam," Jim agreed.

They were both watching him now, as the smell of meat marinated in garlic and herbs and wine began to spread all through the lush green garden. He looked so strong and capable and easy today. If she hadn't known the truth, Meg would have said he was a man who'd never known deep pain, or loss, or fear. He and Connor Callahan were egging each other into some sort of brotherly contest, it looked like.

"Oh, no, not the tree," Meg heard Jim mutter.

"Which tree?" she said.

"That one!" He pointed to the gigantic pine tree, which must have stood in this large, untidy, yet well-loved garden before it even was a garden, when the land around here was used for farming, not houses.

Connor must have dared Adam to have a race to the top, obviously something they'd done as kids a dozen times.

"Jeri, don't encourage them!" Jim muttered again, evidently addressing the twenty-year-old, who must be a cousin of some sort. She was way out of earshot, unfortunately. "Oh, she is, of course! She's worse than they are!"

Jeri had borrowed Adam's watch and was timing the ascent. "On your marks! Get set! Go!" she yelled, and everyone in the garden stopped talking and turned to watch as Adam began to climb one side of the huge trunk while Connor tackled the other. Connor was in the lead immediately, despite a slight limp Meg had noticed when he walked.

"First hand on a branch gets right of way," Connor grunted at Adam.

"Okay, then take your hand off this one, because it's mine, little brother," Adam grunted back, and he stretched one arm up as far as it would go.

Like Connor, Adam was fully aware that they had the whole garden full of people as audience. Unlike Connor, he had no idea, anymore, why he was doing this. For Connor, it was simple. For fun. He liked his risks, did Connor, but he liked them clean and simple, a physical challenge, a chance to pit himself against nature in some way.

Adam admired that, and had shared the craving until a few years ago. These days, he had too much else to consume his will and strength, but it was important to him to retain their connection. Of all his brothers, Connor was perhaps the one he valued most.

And climbing trees was great—liberating, energizing, and just plain exhilarating. More people ought to do it. For the first couple of minutes, he hadn't thought about anything except which branch to reach for next, and how to overtake Connor as the trunk began to thin. It was far too long since he'd been so consumed by a physical task.

But now here he was, approaching the top and thinking, "What if Amy wakes up and I'm not there? What if no one hears her? What if, heaven forbid, I should fall, or something? How can I possibly take risks like this when I have a daughter who needs me so much? Am I crazy?"

His heart had begun to pound, and he was sweating. The only reason he wanted to win, now, was so that he could get this stupid brotherly stunt over and done with and get back to the ground to Amy before something terrible—exactly what, he didn't know— came along and hit him out of the blue.

Both men were out of breath when they reached the top, Connor's head level with Adam's knees and the branches swaying dangerously. Connor was still laughing. Adam wasn't, but he admitted reluctantly "That was...fun, Connor."

The word didn't even sound right in his mouth, it seemed like so long since he'd thought of anything he did in that way. He felt, right now, like a prisoner in solitary confinement might feel if he'd suddenly and unexpectedly, with no prior notice, been taken out into the exercise yard and told to loosen up. Yeah, it was great, but in the back of his mind he could still see the prison bars and feel the walls pressing around him.

Halfway down, a few minutes later, his glance strayed once more to Meg, as it had been doing ever since she'd arrived about half an hour earlier.

I've got to go and talk to her. Even if it's just party stuff, about how I'm glad she came and can I get her something to drink. I'm not fooling her. She knows I've seen her. Every time our eyes meet it's like there's a crashing sound, splintering glass or something. She wants me to talk to her. She's watching me even more than I'm watching her. Doesn't she realize that it'd be crazy of us to follow this...this chemistry between us...where it wants to go? I won't do it!

He hit the ground with a final jump and went to receive Cousin Jeri's accolades on his win, vowing not to look in Meg's direction again until he was actually ready to speak to her.

Over by the barbecue, Jim was saying to Meg, "Did you know he was such an athlete?"

"I had an inkling," she confessed, remembering the six-foot high snow jump on the sledding hill, and the wild fifteen-year-old with red, half-frozen ears and a grin that left no room on his face for anything else. Was that really the same Adam? He hadn't been grinning much on that tree climb just now, after the first few yards. She knew, because she hadn't taken her eyes off him the entire time.

"He's had the worst time of all," Jim said, "but I

have an inkling that maybe he's come to the end of it now.''

''Does *he* think that, I wonder?'' Meg mused aloud.

She'd had a growing sense over the past few days that Adam was locked in a prison of his own making, and that he'd need some cathartic event to shatter those prison walls. One tree climb with his brother wasn't going to do it.

There were times when she wanted to yell at him, ''Snap out of it! *You're* the problem, and you have to be the solution, too.'' Other times, she told herself it wasn't her concern and she was going to keep as far away from Adam Callahan's emotional life as she could possibly get.

''Perhaps not yet,'' Jim answered Meg's question carefully, passing her the marinade to baste the steaks some more. ''But give him time, give him time. Has he seen that you're here yet?''

''Yes, but he hasn't come over.''

''Go over to him.'' He gestured in Adam's direction with a hot dog on a barbecue fork.

''I don't know,'' Meg said. ''It looks like a lot of people want his time, and he doesn't particularly—''

''Go over,'' Jim repeated, stabbing the fork in the air so forcefully that the hot dog flew off and fell on the grass. He ignored it. ''Don't hang back. Don't expect—'' He stopped and began again, still waving the fork. ''How can I put it? Let's just say, accept that there are times with Adam when you're going to have to meet him more than halfway. A lot closer to the pine tree than to the barbecue, for example. That is, if it's important to you to find a meeting point with him in the first place.''

He put the fork down at last and looked at her steadily.

"It is. Oh, it is," she answered, and she knew that for both of them the meaning went deeper than the obvious.

It ought to have been a pretty uncomfortable feeling—that she was emotionally stripped bare in front of the father of the man she loved. Especially with forty uncooked hot dogs as witnesses. But actually, it wasn't uncomfortable at all. She'd come to trust both Jim and Beth since she'd known them, and it was good to feel that they were on her side.

"You could tell everyone over by the pine tree that the steaks are done," Jim suggested.

"But they're not," she pointed out.

"Doesn't matter. It'll take them a couple of minutes to round themselves up and get plates for themselves, anyhow. The steaks'll be done by then."

"So it's just an excuse to go talk to Adam?"

"If you're looking for one, honey," he said casually, putting the hot dogs down on the grill in rows.

"Oh, I am. Thanks, Jim. I might as well be honest about it. I am!"

She set off across the garden, and didn't even see Dad and Patty until she heard Patty's voice at her elbow.

"Hi, Meg. Sorry we're late. Your dad got off at the wrong exit."

They hugged, and Meg didn't admit to her parents that she'd been so busy feeling angry with Adam and having a heart-to-heart with Adam's father that she hadn't even realized how time was passing.

"You haven't missed the food," Meg said. "The

steaks are almost done, and there are snacks on the trestle tables.''

"Chips?" Patty said eagerly. "I really feel like a little salt.''

"Are you feeling okay, Patty?''

"I just can't seem to shake this flu-type feeling. Sometimes I'm fine, but then I get so tired! I guess I'm just getting old, or hitting the change of life a little early, or something, and with this new prospect of moving back east...''

"Go eat some chips, then. You look too thin.''

"We like accusing each other of that, don't we?'' Patty smiled.

"Well, they say giving food or urging someone to eat, is a way of giving love...''

"Meg, what a sweet thing to say to your step-mother!''

Patty hugged her again, with moistening eyes, and Burt took her firmly by the elbow and steered her toward a huge bowl of chips, muttering something about replenishing the salt loss from her tear ducts.

"So, you don't say hello anymore?'' growled Adam a moment later, as Patty and Burt headed for the food tables.

Meg whirled around and glared up at him. "That's rich! That is *rich*, coming from you, Adam Calla-han!'' she exclaimed, giving full vent to all the frus-tration he'd been generating inside her lately. "You're the one who's been shoulder-deep in cous-ins, and brothers, and goodness knows who else!''

"They won't bite.''

"Well, I wouldn't know, would I?'' she retorted, "Since I haven't been introduced!''

He rubbed his chin with his thumb and forefinger,

and looked a little harried. "Okay," he conceded. "You're right."

"So why pretend it was my fault?"

"Attack is the best form of defense?" he suggested hopefully.

"Adam—"

"I've been thinking," he said, as if this was an explanation.

"Poor thing! I hope it didn't hurt too much," she purred with mocking sympathy.

"Don't, Meg."

"I won't, if you won't."

"Won't what?"

"I don't know." She shook her head. "I don't know what we're talking about."

"Then come and see Amy," he offered.

"Oh, is she awake now?"

"Hope not. She's been playing pretty hard since she got home the other day. She fell asleep in the car on the way here half an hour ago. I moved her to the crib, and I'm hoping she'll sleep at least another hour and a half. But I thought it's such a beautiful sight, Amy asleep in a normal crib *without* an IV line in her arm and with some color coming back into her cheeks. I—can't really believe it's real yet, and I thought you might like to see for yourself and…oh, I don't know…pinch me so I know I'm not dreaming."

"Oh, I would! I'd love to see her." She couldn't help adding, "And I guess you won't feel I'm too much of a threat to her when she's asleep!"

"Don't," he said again, as they reached the house and went inside.

This time, she knew *exactly* what he meant, and

retorted, "Why not? It's how you feel, isn't it? No matter what I do or say, you don't trust me, or my parents, and everything becomes fuel for that. Do you know how angry that makes me? And how helpless? And how self-conscious?"

"Meg…"

"It's like I'm permanently hooked up to a lie detector and you're the one controlling the test. Is that ever going to change, Adam?"

"Meg!" They stopped at the foot of the wide wooden stairs and faced each other.

"And is it fair to any of us?" she ploughed on, needing to say all of it. "How can I build a relationship with my niece, my sister's child, if I'm being chaperoned and observed at every moment? Don't you think she's going to start mistrusting me, and Dad and Patty, as she gets older and starts to sense how you're watching us? That kind of thing has to be damaging to her, doesn't it? You're a doctor, you ought to know that better than I do. And Dad and Patty are going to be moving back here to Philadelphia next month. Dad found out two days ago, which means there's absolutely no excuse for you to—"

"Meg Jonas!" he said through clenched teeth as he took her shoulders in his hands. "If you'd let me get a word in edgewise…"

"Okay. Sure! Shoot!" She lifted her chin and narrowed her eyes at him. He needn't think he was going to get around her too easily!

"I told you, I'd been thinking, and I want us to gradually work toward your having a greater involvement in Amy's life."

"You sound like a politician. Go on, use as many words as you can to say nothing at all!"

"Dammit! Okay, then! You can take her out, is what I mean, and your parents, too, since you say they're moving back here. *Without* me tagging along. How about every second weekend, spending an afternoon with her? No sleep-overs, yet. She's too little, and she already stays over at Mom and Dad's a lot. She's woken three times each night, both nights since she's been home, and I don't want her having to adjust to a third room and bed. Okay, so I admit I'm nervous about it, but wouldn't you be?"

"I don't tend to suspect people I like of being kidnappers, strangely enough!"

"I didn't mean that!"

"You did a week ago."

He ignored her. "I'm talking about what any normal parent fears. That she might have some kind of accident while she's in your care and I'd never forgive myself for not being there, and I'd never forgive you for not preventing it, even if I *knew* it wasn't your fault."

"Logical," she commented sarcastically.

"Parenthood isn't logical, Meg," he said fiercely. "It comes from the guts." He took his hand from her shoulder and fisted it against his stomach. "Here. Like all love. It comes from here, and if you don't know that about love, then—then— Hell! *Surely* you know it!" His gaze raked over her, his passion like fire in the depths of his dark eyes. "Surely you know it," he repeated softly. "You *do* know it, don't you, Meg?" he whispered finally, just before their lips met.

"I know it…better…than I want to," she said, between each hot, tender press of his mouth on hers.

"And it's…your fault, Adam," she added, as he parted her lips with his tongue.

"My fault?" Adam just managed to get out. He couldn't believe that they were doing this, locked together like this, when there was so much else they were both feeling. Anger, confusion, who knew what other stuff?

Her arms came round him now, and he returned the gesture, wrapping her tightly against him so that he could feel the soft press of her neat, rounded breasts and the harder nudge of her slim hips.

"Yes, your fault," she said, talking and kissing at the same time.

The effect was fabulous. He felt every movement of her mouth, and the faint whisper of each breath. Fire teased at his groin. He kept going, steadily deepening their kiss, until her head was stretched back and he could move his mouth to run it down her neck and kiss her throat, then explore on down to the upper slopes of her breasts, just hinted at above the round neck of her summery apricot blouse.

"I've always been…sensible…logical," she said, struggling to keep her focus.

It shouldn't make him so happy that he could distort her control this way, but it did. Triumph surged inside him as he realized once and for all that this was no game for her, no strategy. She was as much a prisoner of it as he was.

"Dad taught me that," she went on. He could see how hard she was fighting for coherent speech. "Think before you act. Feel, but be sure that what you're feeling makes sense. And *nothing* about you makes sense, Adam Callahan. I think I hate you. Believe me, I can list *all* of your faults and failings! All the reasons why the last thing I want is to get any closer to you than I have to be. And then this happens, and...and..."

She gave a little whimper of need as he deliberately pressed his thighs against her. He ran his hands down her rear end and kneaded it gently, then slipped his fingers up inside her blouse to touch her, skin to skin. He shuddered. It wasn't enough. He could so easily take this to the very limit of endurance for both of them.

"Adam, please!" she moaned.

"Do you want it to stop?" he demanded huskily, enjoying his sensual power despite every other warring feeling inside him. "Is that what you're saying?"

"Yes... No."

"I'm glad we got *that* cleared up!"

"Well, tell me, Adam..." She pulled away and looked at him, her hair all over her face in a glossy, lacy web, and her fingers linked tightly behind his neck. "Is it different for you? Can you honestly tell me this is *not* the most mixed-up, difficult, *maddening* relationship you've ever had in your life?"

"No, I can't," he admitted. His whole body pulsed.

"So tell me, what's the theory, here?" she whispered. "Since you tell me you understand that love comes from the guts. What do you follow, and what do I follow? What should anyone follow? Their head or their heart?"

"Their heart," he said slowly, watching her mouth, feeling her against him, then losing it, as if she was suddenly separated from him by a chasm filled with mist. "It has to be the heart, doesn't it? So why, I wonder, did Mom spend several thousand words on the phone yesterday convincing me to listen to my head?''

"I don't know," Meg answered, though she'd already realized that he was speaking more to himself now.

Look at those brooding, coffee-black eyes of his, not even seeing her anymore!

Once again, just seconds after they'd shared the kiss of a lifetime, he was struggling painfully with the demons inside him, and she was completely shut out. She would have done anything to have him talk to her about it and ask for her help.

He wouldn't, though. She knew that by now. It was why she'd decided yesterday to put her legal practice on hold for a month while she went to San Francisco to help her parents with their move east and spend some time with old friends. She needed the break! She needed some space, so that she'd have a chance of forgetting what it felt like to love him.

He was frowning now. The softness and heat and triumphant pleasure she'd seen in his face as they kissed had disappeared, and the severe planes and angles she was so familiar with were back in place.

She wanted to shout at him, "Stop it! Just stop whatever it is you're torturing yourself with, because it's *hurting* you! And it's hurting me, too. It's slowly killing off everything we might have been able to build together. Can't you see that? Don't you care? You're tying yourself in knots over nothing, and for some reason you keep pushing me away so that I'm powerless to help you. I've racked my brains over this, I've lain awake at night, but there just isn't anywhere left for me to go. If you don't trust me now, if you don't *want* what you feel about me after what we've been through over the past few weeks, then I can't see that you ever will.''

But she didn't say any of this. With a growing feeling of total helplessness, she sensed that he was already miles away.

"Is that Amy I can hear?" he asked, lifting his head to try and hear a sound from upstairs.

Meg shook her head. "I can't tell. I can't hear anything, except for party noise from outside."

"I think it is. Maybe she's had a bad dream." He started up the stairs, taking them two at a time.

She followed him, not knowing if he still wanted her to see Amy or not.

"I'm coming, honey," he called softly.

Behind him, Meg still couldn't hear anything, even when she was walking across the landing at the top of the stairs to the door of the spare room. This was effectively Amy's room now, since she'd been staying here at her grandparents' house so often. When Meg entered the room, Adam was already standing beside the crib, frowning down at it. Inside, his little girl was fast asleep, her dark lashes fanning across her cheeks and a little smile hovering on her face.

"I don't understand it," Adam said. "I'm sure I heard her crying."

He reached into her crib and put a finger against the side of her neck.

"What are you doing, Adam?" Meg asked.

"Checking her pulse, of course."

She stared at him. "Isn't that a little unnecessary? She's fine, isn't she?"

"Yes, but..." He trailed off and frowned once more, then looked down at his own hand, still touching Amy's neck. "I—" He shook his head. "I guess

I do this a lot. It's a sort of reflex, just to check. But…'' Again, he didn't finish, and shook his head, more forcefully this time, as if to clear away cobwebs. ''She's fine,'' he finished at last. ''Of course. She's fine.''

''She's beautiful,'' Meg said, coming closer. ''You were right. It is a treat just to see her like this, so normal. I—I love her, Adam. Is it okay to say that?''

''The more people that love her, the better!'' he answered lightly. ''Still, I think I'm probably the only one who hallucinates her crying!'' He stayed watching the sleeping child in silence for some time.

When they went downstairs some minutes later, they still hadn't spoken. Something didn't feel right, Meg decided. Adam hadn't ''hallucinated'' Amy's cry, he'd just made a mistake. Easy enough to do, with the party noise going on outside, but for some reason the mistake seemed significant and it seemed to Meg that despite the heat of the kiss they'd shared, she was farther from a complete connection with him than ever.

Chapter Ten

"I'm sorry," Patty apologized shakily, as Meg and Adam met her and Burt in the kitchen. Patty looked sick as she held her husband's arm. "I just threw up behind a forsythia bush. It was the French onion dip. It just tasted...weird."

"Would you like to come through and lie down on the couch?" Adam offered at once.

"Yes, please! And, Meg, honey, could you get me a glass of water?"

"Of course, Patty."

Burt and Adam settled Patty on the couch while Meg brought the water, and the green tinge soon ebbed from Patty's skin. But Meg's father was still concerned.

"We've got to do something about this, Patty!" he said, crouching beside her and taking her hand in his. "We've got to stop making excuses. Adam, she needs to see a doctor, doesn't she?"

Adam studied her thoughtfully. "You know, I

think she probably does," he answered finally. "But, Patty, I'd say maybe you want to do a pregnancy test first."

"A pregnancy test? Oh, my lord!" she gasped, struggling to sit up again on the overstuffed floral-patterned couch. "Is *that* what all this is? But I couldn't be! I'm almost forty-five!"

"It wouldn't be the first time. Would you like to be pregnant?" Adam asked.

"Oh, it'd be the most wonderful miracle in the world!" she said, and burst into tears yet again.

Half an hour later, Adam's suggestion was confirmed. Unable to wait, Patty and Meg's father had driven to the nearest drugstore to buy a testing kit, and after a short time in the bathroom, Patty emerged to announce the result, "Positive! And the testing strip went a real dark purple. Is that good?"

"That's great," Adam told her.

After this, he found himself undergoing the hero treatment to an almost embarrassing degree. Both Patty and Burt were walking on air, and the whole Callahan clan, once the news spread, started treating it like an extra reason to celebrate.

"As if we needed it!" Beth said, piling her plate with a second helping of barbecue.

"I guess it explains why I've been so emotional lately!"

"It's a well-known side effect," Adam agreed. For some reason, her happiness was making him uncomfortable. Did she know what she was in for?

"Do you know, Adam I got so crazy at times, I even talked about kidnapping your little girl!" Patty went on.

"I know," he answered calmly, and saw her eyes widen with surprise.

"Meg told you that?" She glanced sideways at her stepdaughter.

"I overheard her talking to you about it on the phone," Adam said.

"Believe me, once I'd met you I realized it wouldn't be necessary, not to mention the fact that Meg tried to talk me out of it from the beginning, didn't you, Meg?"

"I did, only I doubt that Adam wants to hear me say so yet again," was her double-edged answer.

She wasn't eating, and she looked exhausted and unhappy, Adam realized, though he could tell how gallantly she was working to hide it so that she didn't smudge the clear light of her parents' happiness. She was an incredibly loyal daughter.

Distantly, he appreciated what a great quality that was. Emotionally, it didn't have the power to touch him at all today, and when she announced a little later that she was going home, he didn't make any attempt to stop her. The fight in him just seemed to have gone.

Burt Jonas came up to Adam as he watched Meg say her thanks and goodbyes to his mother. Mom asked a question. Adam thought he saw the word "Amy" on her lips. Meg smiled and nodded as she replied, but he couldn't work out what she was saying.

"She's going home," Burt commented unnecessarily, watching his daughter as intently as Adam was.

"I know."

"Are you going to do anything about that?"

"What do you mean?"

"I mean, go after her, talk to her."

"Uh, no, I don't think so."

"In that case," Burt went on calmly, in a conversational tone, "I can't decide if I should simply kill you on the spot, or drag you to her by your collar and pin you to the ground with my shoe on the back of your neck until you're ready to tell her how you feel. She's not going to wait, Adam. I know my daughter, and if she doesn't believe there's any hope, any prospect of something good coming out of what she feels, she'll bail out now before she gets in still deeper, and she'll start doing what she needs to do to heal herself. Believe that! And if that's *not* what she should be doing, then she needs to hear it from you."

A leaden weight settled in Adam's stomach, and he didn't bother to feel any surprise that Meg's father should have read him so clearly.

"I hate how I feel," he said.

"And why is that?"

"Because I don't trust it. I don't trust anything, anymore."

Again, Burt Jonas simply asked, "Why?"

"It seems so much safer that way. And speaking of safety, can't you get Patty to ground herself a little? Shouldn't you remind her about the risk of a first pregnancy at her age? I can't stand to see her looking so happy!"

"Oh, lord, you've really got a bad case, haven't you?" Meg's father sighed. "Look at her, Adam, just look at my wife!"

"She's not touching the ground," he agreed.

"I know, and do you think I want to take that away from her now, just because it might not last forever? Isn't that all the more reason to truly feel it *now*? She's having a baby, Adam. It's all she's ever wanted, and now it's happening, and babies are the purest form of happiness on earth, as far as I'm concerned. I've had two of 'em, and with all the hurt I've had over Cherie, do you think I'd wish she'd never been born? Not for a second! Isn't that how your parents feel, with all eight of you? And isn't it how you feel about Amy, even with everything you've been through?''

"Of course," Adam said. "It *was* how I felt. It *is*," he added more firmly. "Of course it is!''

"And do you really want to lose something so precious from your life *now*, before you've even had a chance to experience it properly, just because it doesn't come with iron-clad guarantees of safety?''

"I—I— That's an interesting question, Mr. Jonas. It's not one I've allowed myself to consider.''

And all at once he started to feel like there was a fog lifting all around him, changing a cold misty dawn into a bright warm day. What he wanted, and what was possible, suddenly became a whole lot clearer.

"Then *do* consider it," Burt suggested softly. "Think about it for a minute, then tell me how you really feel about my daughter and what you're going to do about it.''

"I don't need to think about it," Adam said, a new energy and determination rippling through him. "That's the last thing I need to do! Because you're absolutely right. Hell, it's so obvious! Will you excuse me for a while? I have to go catch up to Meg.''

"I will not cry about this!" Meg vowed to herself as she left the Callahan family home and began to walk down the street to where her car was parked.

"There's no point. It goes beyond tears. I've made a decision, and I'll feel strong about that if it kills me!"

She didn't take any notice of the sound of a car starting up somewhere behind her. It was a long street, tree-lined and pretty, with summer annuals in flower in all the gardens and the sound of birds in the shrubbery. With the large gathering in attendance at the Callahans, she'd had to park quite a distance away, in the direction of the park she and Adam had taken Amy to that day weeks ago. She didn't mind the walk. It was a good way to vent feelings, and to energize her anger.

I'm right to be angry, she decided. He knows how I feel about him. I've practically said it straight out. And I know what he could feel...what he *does* feel...for me. Only he won't act on it! I'm not asking for the moon. All I want is some acknowledgment from him that he's prepared to take just one tiny little risk for the sake of what we could have together, but he won't. He won't even begin to explore it, and without that, without even a beginning, I'm just not going to hang around waiting to get hurt!

A month in California probably wouldn't be nearly enough, but it was the very most she could afford to take off from her law practice. Even so, she'd be on the phone first thing on Monday morning to a couple of colleagues in the area, giving them some of her upcoming real estate closings. No doubt about it, she'd lose business through this, but it couldn't be helped. When the ship starts to sink, you take to the lifeboats. Simple as that. No matter what the other costs might be.

"I should send him an invoice," she decided, "For

every penny this is going to cost me.'' As if the financial cost was remotely an issue!

Oh, hell, and now she *was* crying, even though she'd vowed not to!

And there seemed to be some car cruising up behind her, very slowly, as she marched down the street. If its driver wanted anything more than directions to the nearest Interstate, he was in for an unpleasant surprise.

She wheeled around, hands on hips, ready to tell an intrusive stranger that, no, she did not need a ride, thanks, but the words died on her lips.

''I was just wondering,'' Adam said, leaning back in the seat of an open-topped car, pushing up silver-lensed sunglasses and studying her intently, ''if you've ever been for a ride in a red Corvette on a warm spring afternoon.''

''No, I haven't. And you don't *have* a red Corvette. Did you steal it or something?''

''It's Connor's. I borrowed it.''

''I'm very happy for you. Now, if you'll excuse me, this is my car right here, and—''

''Heck, Meg, I know I deserve this, but—''

''Say that again?'' He'd caught her attention now. She didn't put her car key back in her pocket…but she didn't put it into the lock, either.

''I deserve it,'' he repeated seriously. ''Now, will you please get into this vehicle before I—''

''And once more, for good luck,'' she suggested very firmly.

''*I deserve it,* okay? So can I take you for a nice fast drive, with a picnic and a bottle of champagne at the end of it, and can we talk?''

''A picnic.''

"You didn't eat anything at the barbecue."

"You noticed?"

"I notice an awful lot about you, Meg Jonas," he answered. "I have from the very beginning, even when I didn't want to. Look, I threw some of the barbecue food in some containers, and I already had champagne in my car. I moved it—and me, and the barbecue—to Connor's car, because Connor's car is more fun."

"You keep champagne in your car?"

"Another leftover," he said. "From a few weeks ago, when I thought I wanted to celebrate, then I realized I didn't."

"How come?"

"I didn't want to celebrate with you."

"There's a flaw in your thinking, Adam. Because now you're suggesting—"

"That we celebrate together? Yes! Because Meg, my darling, there have been so many flaws in my thinking just lately that I probably should have gone back and repeated kindergarten."

"Am I going to be sorry that I said yes to this?" she asked with a sigh.

He'd stopped the car in the middle of the road. She'd put her car key away. Now he was reaching across to open the passenger door for her with a huge grin on his face. She'd seen that grin, that same utterly pure, utterly joyous grin, just once before, about sixteen years ago on a wet, half-frozen and very happy teenager, sledding in the snow.

"Sorry?" he said softly. She was seated now, within easy reach of his kiss. It came, whisper-soft, then he pulled away just far enough to look into her eyes. "I don't think so. My mom and dad don't seem to think so. Your dad may kill me if you don't say yes, so if you do…"

"Do what?"

"Say no. Then please tell him before he does—"

"Kill you?"

"Exactly!—that it's really not my fault!"

"Even though you deserve it."

"Even though I deserve it. I thought we'd gotten past that bit."

"I just wanted to recap a little," she said. "You know, 'previously, on the Meg and Adam Show, Adam admits he deserves it.'"

"Yeah, but if we're going to do that, I think we need to recap on an earlier episode."

"Which one?"

"The one where Adam forgets how to trust, because it seems like everything that's important to him gets taken away, and because even the good news has a sting in its tail, and because this fabulous new person in his life might not be who she seems."

"I think I must have missed that episode," Meg said.

"Would you like me to tell you more about what happened in it?"

"Yes, please."

He didn't, though, not just then. Instead, they drove: along some suburban streets until they reached the entrance ramp for the Interstate, down the Interstate just a tiny bit over the speed limit, with the warm afternoon air combing through their hair, across an overpass and back the way they'd just come, which brought a questioning look from Meg.

"Are we actually going someplace?"

"Nope."

"Then—"

"Damned cobwebs in the brain," Adam explained solemnly. "Only way to get them out. Thank goodness Connor has an open-topped car, or it might have been fatal."

"That's what I was afraid of," Meg agreed just as solemnly.

When they'd parked the car and were picnicking in the park they'd been to with Amy, they were both ready to talk about it more seriously.

"It's like I've been in prison," Adam said, lying back on the picnic blanket and pillowing her head on his chest. "Surrounded by these huge, thick walls of fear and distrust."

"I've sensed that."

"It started with all the real reasons I had for fearing I'd lose Amy, and then it just began to spread. I didn't trust anyone or anything anymore, least of all my own perceptions and feelings. Like today, when I actually checked her pulse after I'd thought I heard her crying. I realized that's a reflex now. I've been doing that several times a night, creeping in to check that my daughter's still breathing. It was crazy!

"Mom was telling me yesterday to go with my head not my heart, and that seemed wrong to me, until I realized that what was filling my heart was fear. I *know* now...I've known for days, maybe weeks...that I had no good reason to distrust you. My head had been telling me that, but my gut has gotten so in the habit of it, like an animal that's been mistreated... Sorry, this isn't making sense."

"It is, Adam," she whispered, stroking her fingers down his chest. "It is, and I should have understood just how hard it was for you, but instead I've been angry and impatient.''

"You had every right to be, the way I've treated you. And I have no right, no right at all, to ask you to love me, but I'm asking, anyway. Do you think you could possibly love me, Meg Jonas, the way I love you? I know I've made it hard work for you—''

"Hard work?'' she laughed, propping up on her elbow and leaning across to nuzzle her nose against his.

She hardly dared to believe this was real. Even when she'd climbed into Connor's car with Adam, all she'd been hoping for was a beginning. Not this. *Nothing* like this. He was offering her his whole heart on a plate, as if it was the easiest thing in the world.

And it was.

"You think loving you, knowing now that you love me, will be hard work? Adam Callahan, I could do it in my sleep!''

Epilogue

"I remember this building!" said a bright little voice in the passenger seat behind Adam as he turned into the gloom of a large, multistoried parking garage on a clear September morning.

"You *remember* it?" He threw Amy an astonished glance via the rear-view mirror.

Surely it wasn't possible! It was over two years now since Amy's discharge from this hospital. Then, she'd been just fifteen months old. Now, she was three and a half, with a full head of dark, silky curls, and he and Meg never talked about her illness. They didn't need to. It was a nightmare from the past, and had nothing to do with the present.

Could Amy really still have memories of all the time she'd spent here?

"Yes, Daddy, don't you remember?" she answered rather impatiently. "Mommy and I came here to look at all the babies, and for me to practice being a big sister. It was quite a long time ago," she added kindly. "Maybe you forgot."

"Oh, right," he nodded, relieved at the innocence of her response. No, she shared none of those gut-wrenching memories, and she'd been calling Meg "Mommy" for as long as she could remember. "Of course you did," he went on. "And you got a certificate."

The rectangle of a pale yellow card was still pinned with a ladybug magnet to the refrigerator door in the kitchen in the big new house he and Meg had bought last year. Meg had taken Amy along to a class in "Prepared Sibhood" here at the hospital about three weeks ago, and Amy had come home full of stories about holding a doll baby and changing its diaper and seeing a hospital room "like Mommy's going to have."

She had spent the past five months in a semi-constant state of excitement about the prospect of the new baby, yet now that it was actually here, she was having trouble taking it in.

"Did the baby *really* come out of Mommy's tummy?"

"Yes, honey, in the middle of the night when you were asleep."

"And is Mommy in her room at the hospital now?"

"Yes, she is."

"How are we going to find it? I can't remember which button to press in the elevator, and you didn't come with us to look at the babies before."

"But I used to work at this hospital, Amy, so I

know exactly which button to press to get to the mommies and babies," he told her. "It's Level Six. This one. Can you press it for me?"

She stuck her finger out, taking the important task very seriously, to the point where she must have pressed the button at least eight times.

"That's enough, now, honey."

Adam didn't work here anymore, but had set up a private pediatric practice of his own. It was doing so well that he was about to take on his second associate. Meg had also taken on an associate at her law practice very soon after their wedding two years ago, when she'd made the decision to spend as much time as she could at home with Amy.

There had been no question of Amy going back into childcare, even once she was one hundred percent fit. With Beth and Patty fighting in a comical and completely friendly way about which days of the week they'd each spend with Amy, Meg had had no choice but to cut down to part-time hours. "Otherwise those two grandmothers will fill up the entire calendar, and you and I will be lucky if we get to give Amy her breakfast!"

Amy took all the to-ing and fro-ing between loving arms with the serenity of a retired movie star getting chauffeured between talk show appearances. Adam loved her confidence, loved the willing arms she always held out for a hug. There could be no harm in a child knowing she was loved and wanted by so many people.

The birth of Patty's own little daughter when Amy was still less than two years old hadn't changed anything, nor did the rather exhausting presence of Tom and Julie's active twin girls whenever they came to visit Beth and Jim. There was room for all of them in everybody's hearts.

And since the previous generation of Callahans had all been boys, no one seemed to care too much that the pattern had reversed itself in this next generation, giving Adam, to date, two nieces, one daughter and a toddling half-sister-in-law.

Correction. Until last night the pattern had been reversed. Adam grinned. In about a minute, he'd see the little being who, since exactly eighteen minutes past eleven yesterday evening, had become his favorite male creature in the entire universe. Funny, he hadn't realized until last night just what a beautiful word those three small letters could make: *b-o-y.*

Little James Burton Callahan was nursing at his mother's breast when Adam and Amy came through the doorway. Adam felt his breath catch in his throat. They were both so beautiful.

Hearing footsteps on the carpet, Meg looked up and smiled, still holding the baby against the nourishing warmth of her breast. She looked a little tired, but she had her hair freshly brushed and clipped back. She was wearing the white cotton and lace nightgown that Adam had given her.

His heart swelled, and for a long moment he simply couldn't speak. *So* beautiful! Sometimes he still couldn't work out how he'd gotten to this point, how either of them had managed to cling on to what they felt through the wild ride of those first frightening and painful weeks.

Amy was far more at ease with her emotions. "Is that my new baby brother?" she said as she marched into the room and up to the bed. "Oh, Mommy, Daddy, he's *adorable!*"

"Isn't he though?" Adam whispered.

He reached the bedside and bent to kiss his wife. "Thank you," he said.

He took the gold and sapphire necklace that he'd bought her from his pocket as he spoke, and threaded it around her pretty neck, grinning at her speechless reaction.

"I don't need this," she protested, finding her voice again at last. "Don't you know that this is already the happiest day of my life? I can't vouch for what will happen now that it's gotten even better!"

"*I* needed it," he answered seriously. "To thank you."

"But for what, my darling?"

"For everything you've given me since the day we met. For James, last night. For our marriage two years ago. For my ability to believe in happy endings again. And for Amy's life, first of all. With all my love."

"But, no, you're wrong, Adam," Meg whispered, taking one hand from the baby to thread her fingers back through Adam's hair and pull him closer once more. "Don't thank me for Amy. We both should thank *her* for bringing us together. Without Amy, and, yes, her illness right here in this hospital, that caused us all such pain, it could never have happened."

They both turned to look at their healthy girl and she gave a big sigh. "Go on. It's okay. I don't mind."

"Don't mind what, honey?" Adam said.

"If you kiss Mommy again. I'm quite used to it by now, 'cuz you do it all the time!"

* * * * *

Who's teaching who? Allie Todd needs Connor Callahan's help in learning to be a mom, but in the process she teaches him more about love than he'd ever thought possible. Don't miss their romance, coming only from Silhouette Romance in late 2000.

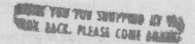

VIRGIN BRIDES

Join
Silhouette Romance
as the New Year brings new
virgin brides down the aisle!

On Sale December 1999
THE BRIDAL BARGAIN
by Stella Bagwell (SR #1414)

On Sale February 2000
WAITING FOR THE WEDDING
by Carla Cassidy (SR #1426)

On Sale April 2000
HIS WILD YOUNG BRIDE
by Donna Clayton (SR #1441)

Watch for more **Virgin Brides** stories from
your favorite authors later in 2000!

VIRGIN BRIDES
only from

Silhouette®
Where love comes alive™

Available at your favorite retail outlet.

Visit us at www.romance.net

SRVB00

Look Who's Celebrating Our 20th Anniversary:

Celebrate 20 YEARS

"Happy 20th birthday, Silhouette. You made the writing dream of hundreds of women a reality. You enabled us to give [women] the stories [they] wanted to read and helped us teach [them] about the power of love."

—*New York Times* bestselling author
Debbie Macomber

"I wish you continued success, Silhouette Books.... Thank you for giving me a chance to do what I love best in all the world."

—International bestselling author
Diana Palmer

"A visit to Silhouette is a guaranteed happy ending, a chance to touch magic for a little while.... It refreshes and revitalizes and makes us feel better.... I hope Silhouette goes on forever."

—Award-winning bestselling author
Marie Ferrarella

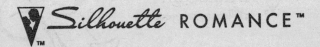
▼ *Silhouette* ROMANCE™

Visit us at www.romance.net

PS20SRAQ1

Multi-*New York Times* bestselling author

NORA ROBERTS

knew from the first how to capture readers' hearts.
Celebrate the 20th Anniversary of Silhouette Books
with this special 2-in-1 edition containing her fabulous
first book and the sensational sequel.

Coming in June

IRISH HEARTS

Adelia Cunnane's fiery temper sets proud, powerful horse
breeder Travis Grant's heart aflame and he resolves to
make this wild *Irish Thoroughbred* his own.

Erin McKinnon accepts wealthy Burke Logan's loveless
proposal, but can this ravishing *Irish Rose* win her
hard-hearted husband's love?

*Also available in June from
Silhouette Special Edition (SSE #1328)*

IRISH REBEL

In this brand-new sequel to *Irish Thoroughbred*, Travis and
Adelia's innocent but strong-willed daughter Keeley discovers
love in the arms of a charming Irish rogue with a talent for
horses...and romance.

Where love comes alive™